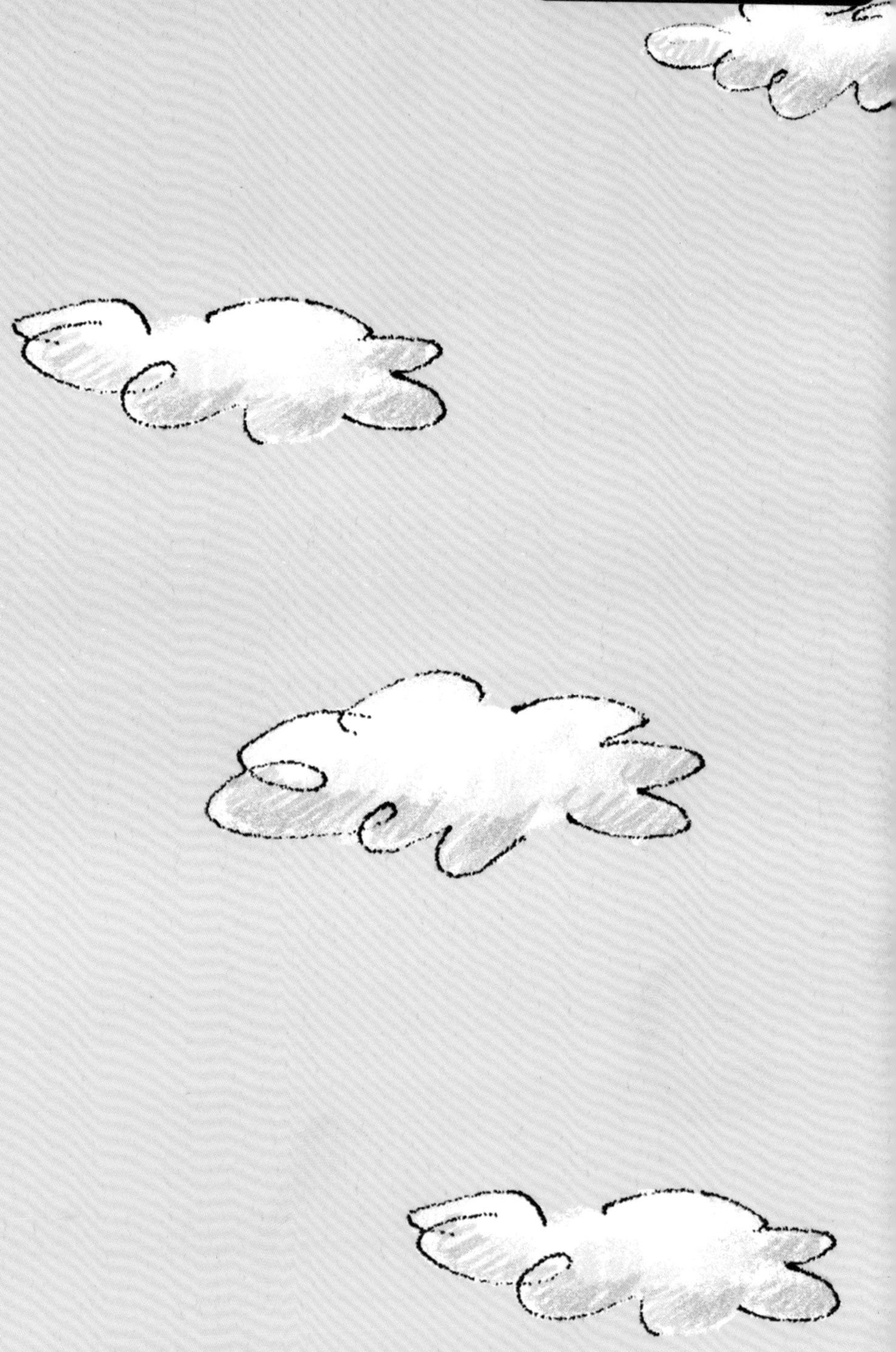

I Like to Read® Comics instill confidence and the joy of reading in new readers. Created by award-winning artists as well as talented newcomers, these imaginative books support beginners' reading comprehension with extensive visual support.

We want to hear every new reader say, "I like to read comics!"

Visit our website for flash cards, activities, and more about the series:
www.holidayhouse.com/ILiketoRead
#ILTR

BOOM!

Paul Meisel

Theodor Seuss Geisel Honoree

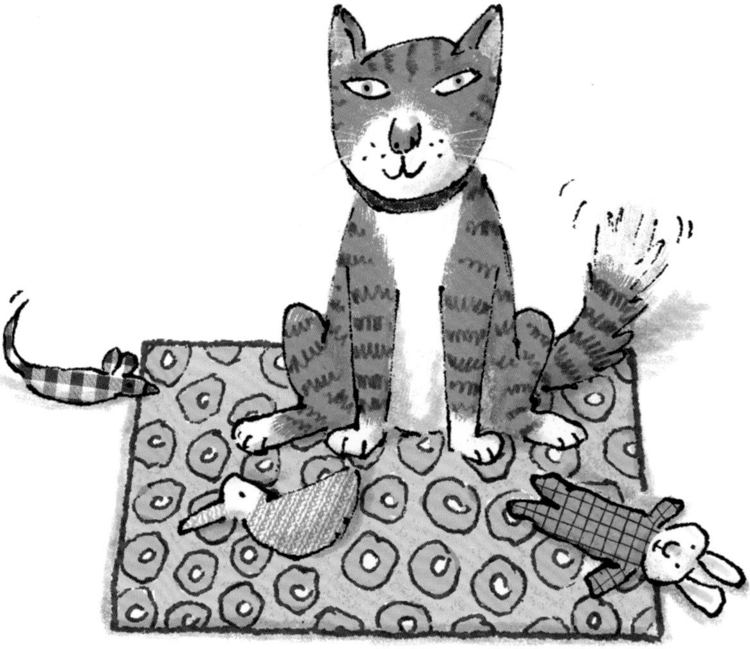

I Like to Read® COMICS

HOLIDAY HOUSE • NEW YORK

RUMBLE RUMBLE

I LIKE TO READ is a registered trademark of Holiday House Publishing, Inc.

Text and illustrations copyright © 2023 by Paul Meisel
All Rights Reserved
HOLIDAY HOUSE is registered in the U.S. Patent and Trademark Office.
Printed and bound in February 2023 at C&C Offset, Shenzhen, China.
The artwork was created with a Mont Blanc Diplomat Fountain Pen with
Higgins Black Magic Ink and FW Acrylic Ink on Saunders Waterford
Cold Press Paper digitally enhanced in Photoshop.
www.holidayhouse.com
First Edition
1 3 5 7 9 10 8 6 4 2

Library of Congress Cataloging-in-Publication Data
Names: Meisel, Paul, author, illustrator.
Title: BOOM! / Paul Meisel.
Description: First edition. | New York: Holiday House, 2023. | Series:
I like to read comics | Audience: Ages 4-8. | Audience: Grades K-1.
Summary: "When a thunderstorm comes, Cat is happy to spend
the noisy night playing with toys, while Dog frantically tries
to find just the right hiding spot"—Provided by publisher.
Identifiers: LCCN 2022031118 | ISBN 9780823448579 (hardcover)
Subjects: LCSH: Cats—Comic books, strips, etc. | Cats—Juvenile fiction.
Dogs—Comic books, strips, etc. | Dogs—Juvenile fiction. | Thunderstorms—Comic
books, strips, etc. | Thunderstorms—Juvenile fiction. | Fear—Comic books, strips, etc.
Fear—Juvenile fiction. | Graphic novels. | CYAC: Graphic novels. | Cats—Fiction.
Dogs—Fiction. | Thunderstorms—Fiction. | Fear—Fiction. | LCGFT: Graphic novels.
Classification: LCC PZ7.7.M4495 Bo 2023 | DDC 741.5/973—dc23/eng/20220808
LC record available at https://lccn.loc.gov/2022031118

ISBN: 978-0-8234-4857-9 (hardcover)

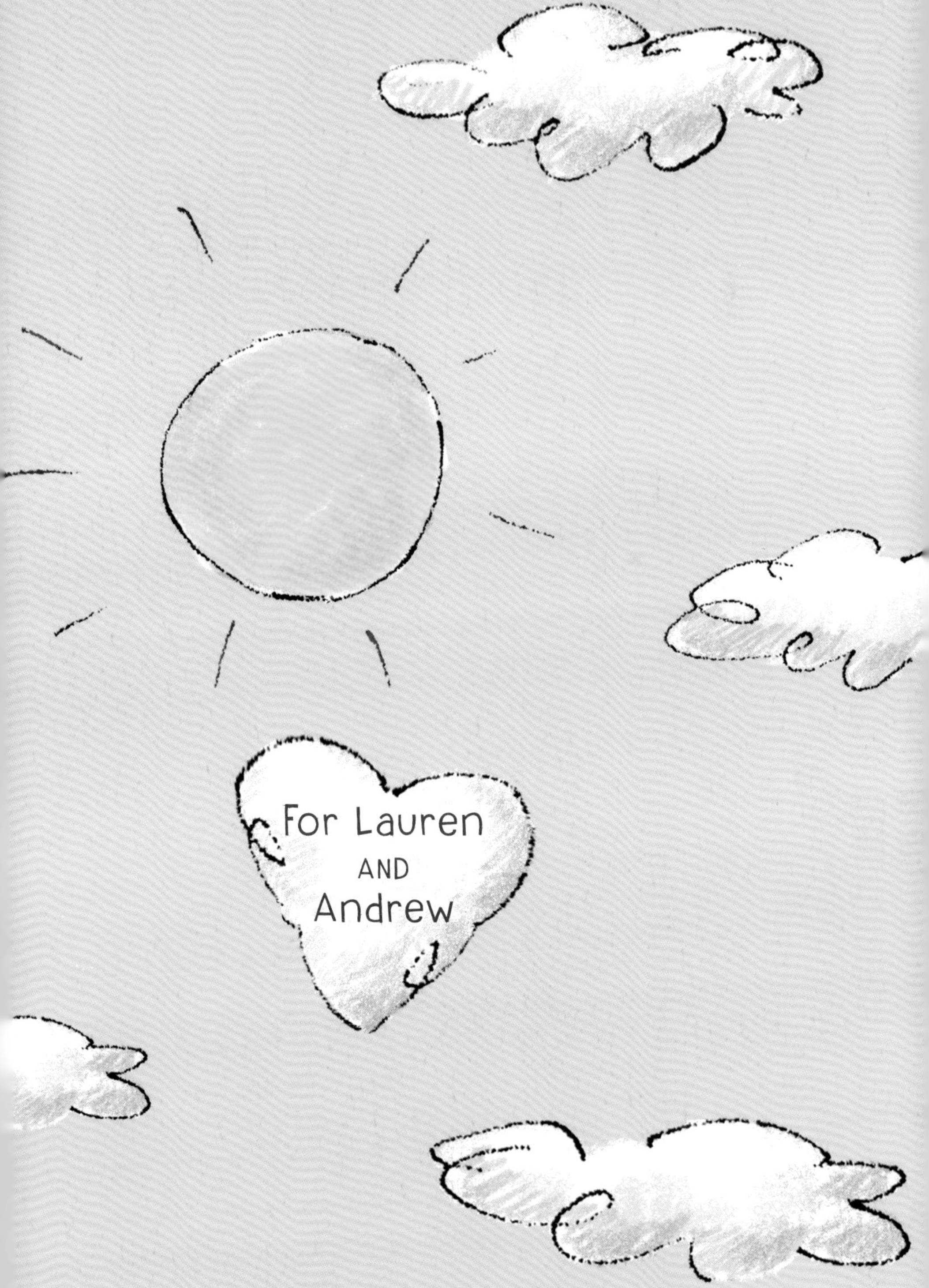

For Lauren
AND
Andrew

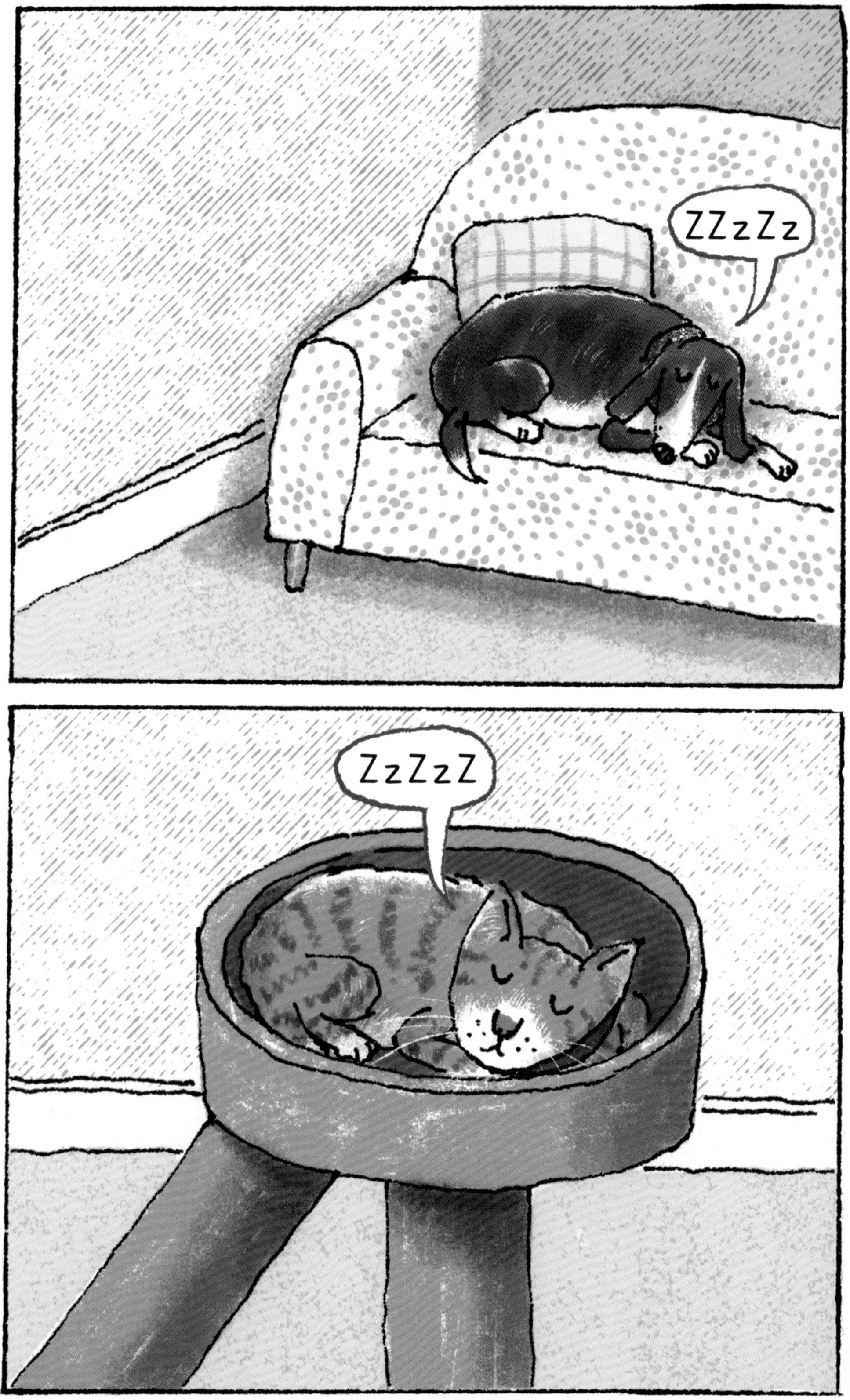
ZZzZz
ZzZzZ

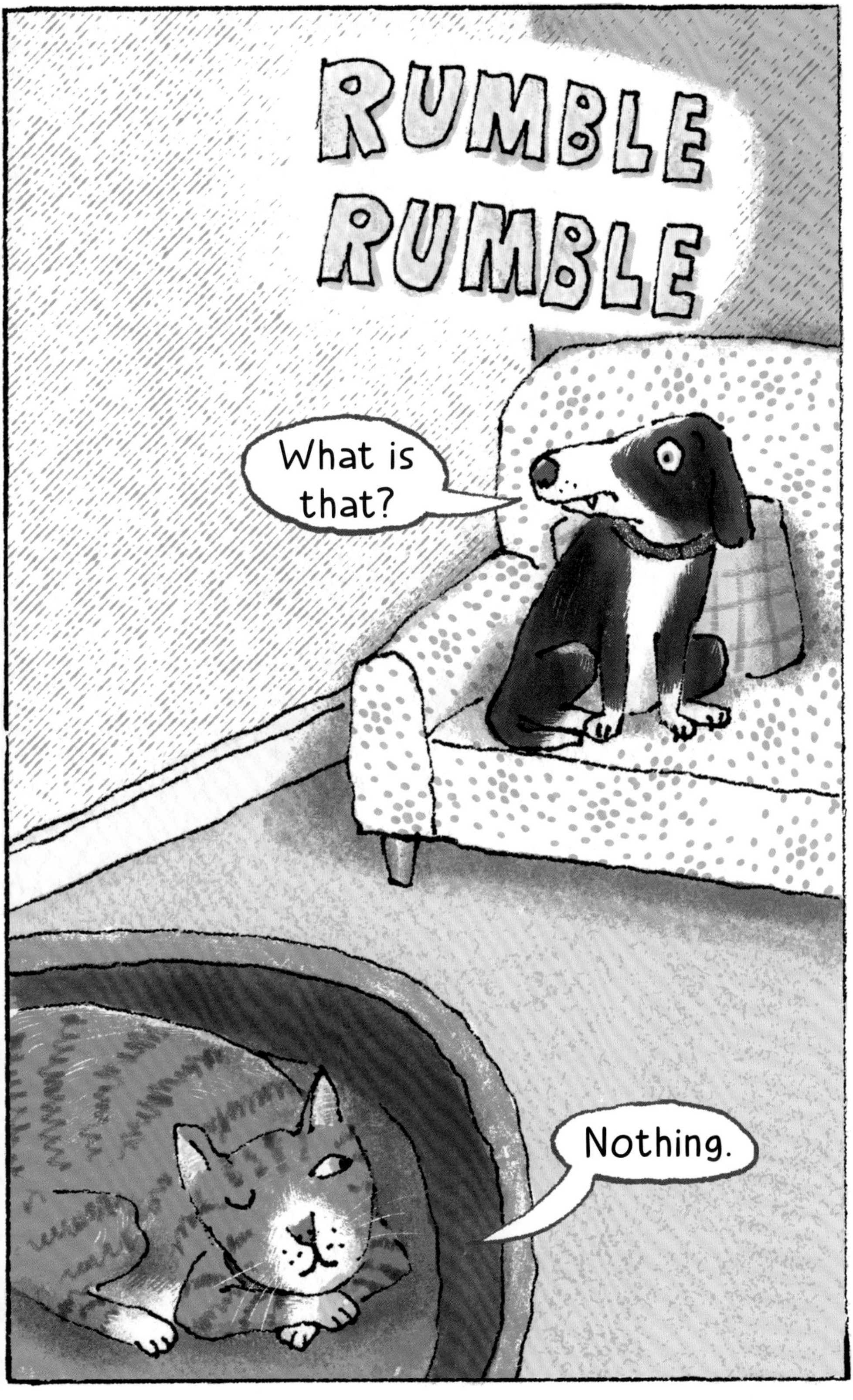
RUMBLE
RUMBLE
What is that?
Nothing.

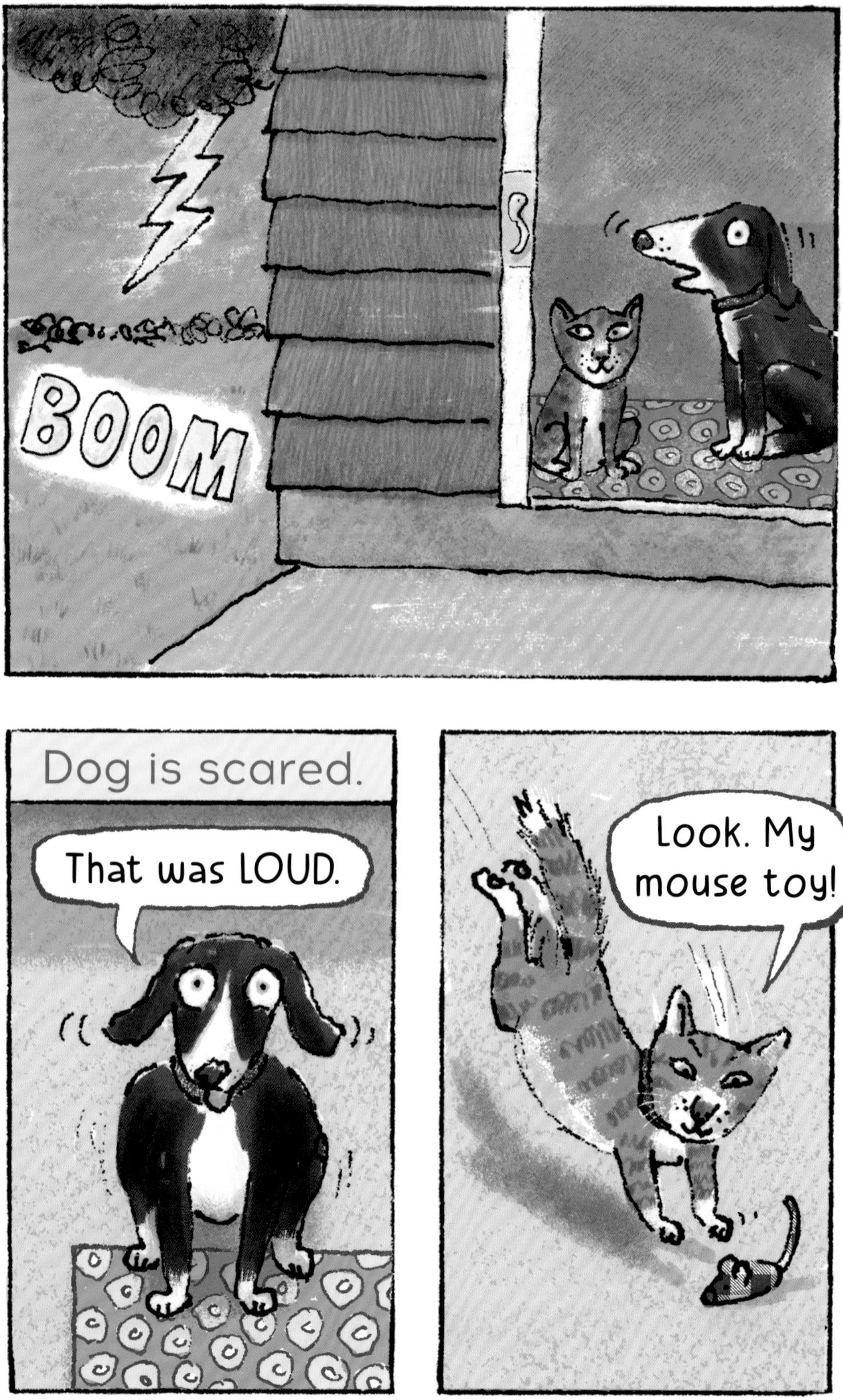
BOOM
Dog is scared.
That was LOUD.
Look. My mouse toy!

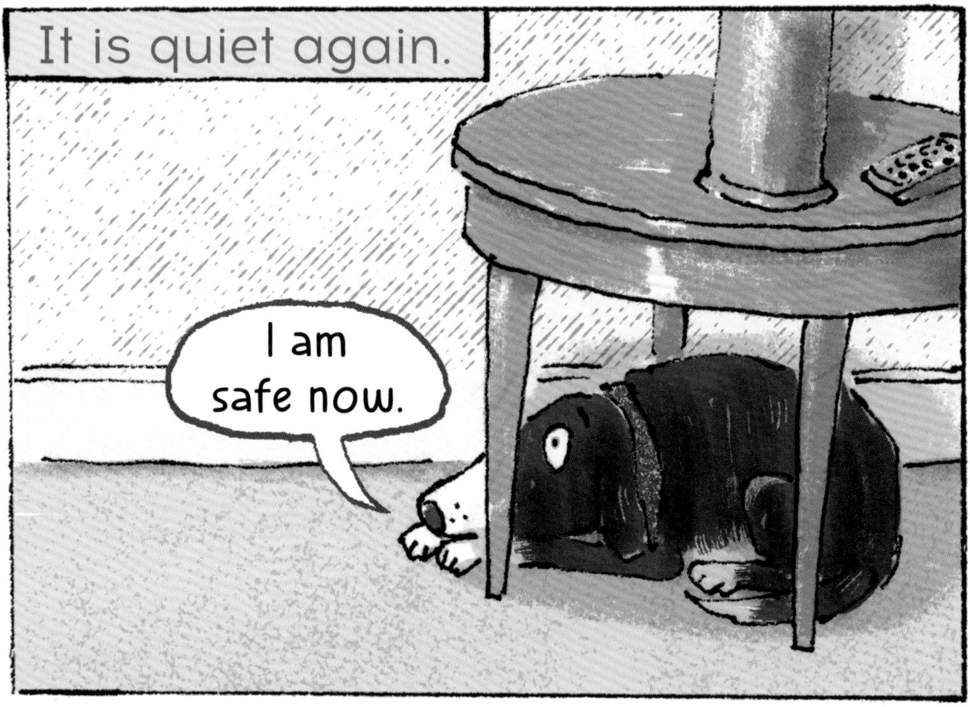
It is quiet again.
I am safe now.

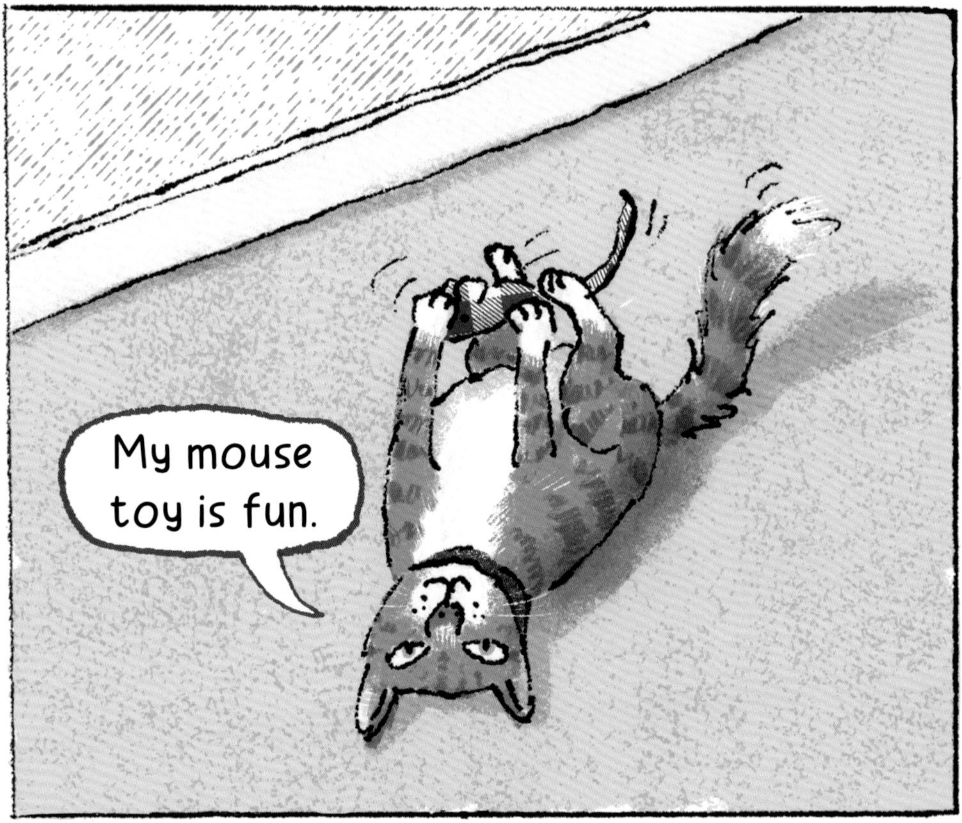
My mouse toy is fun.

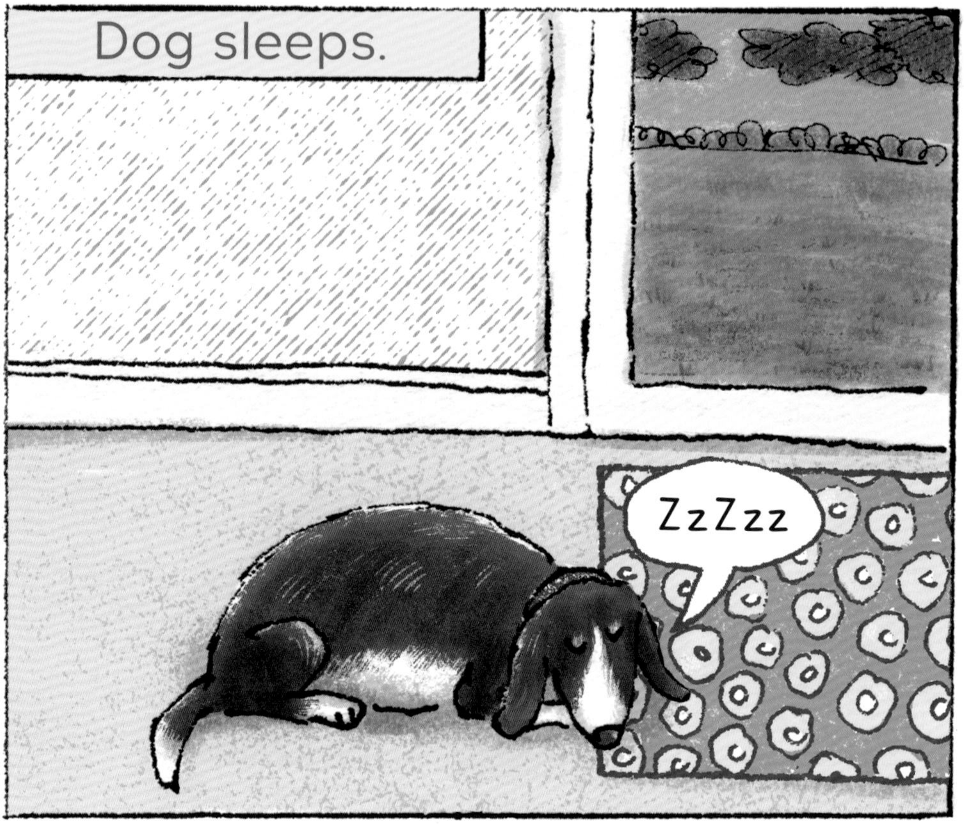
Dog sleeps.
ZzZzz

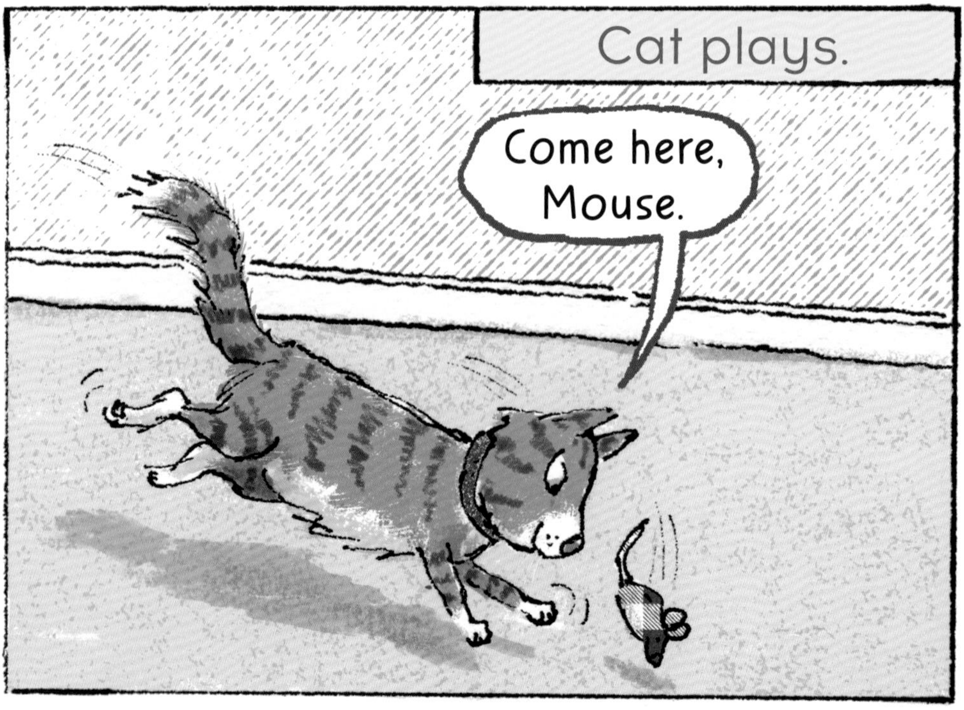
Cat plays.
Come here, Mouse.

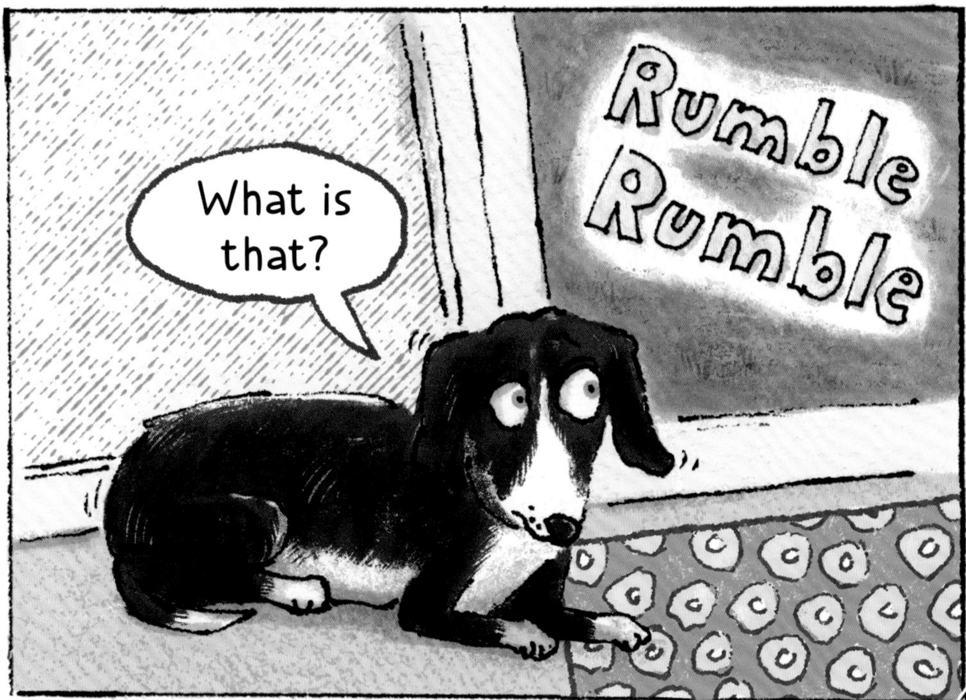
What is that?
Rumble Rumble

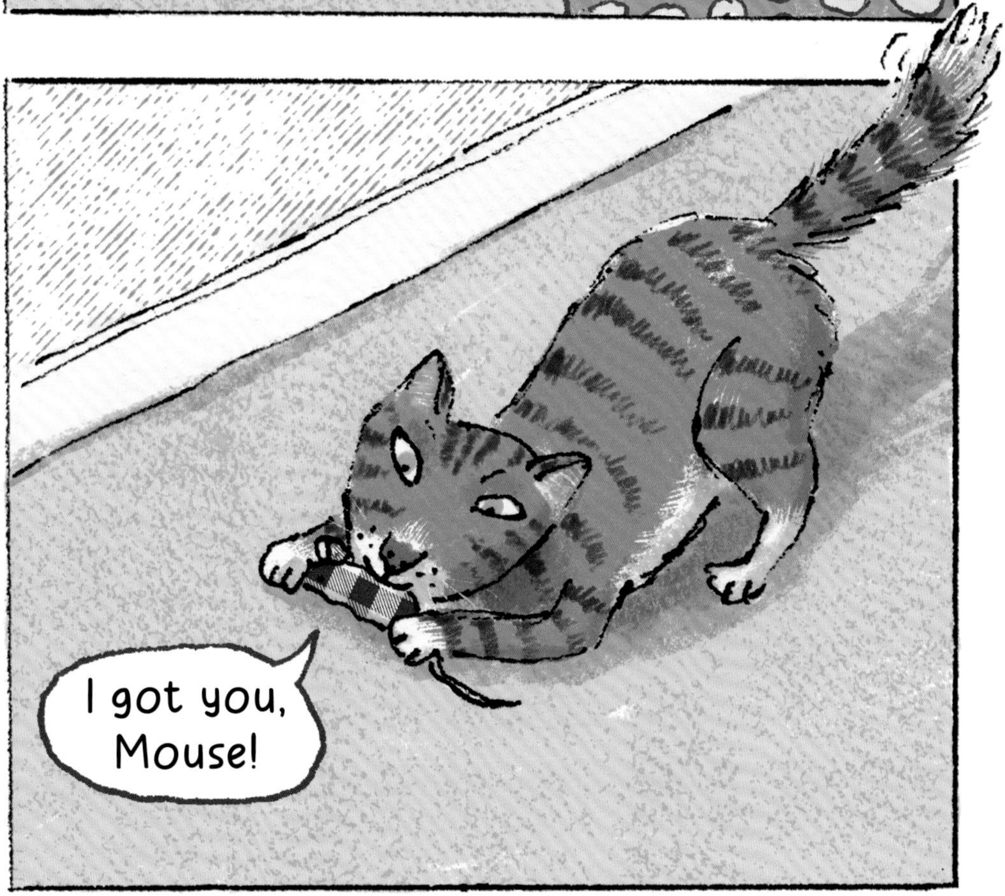
I got you, Mouse!

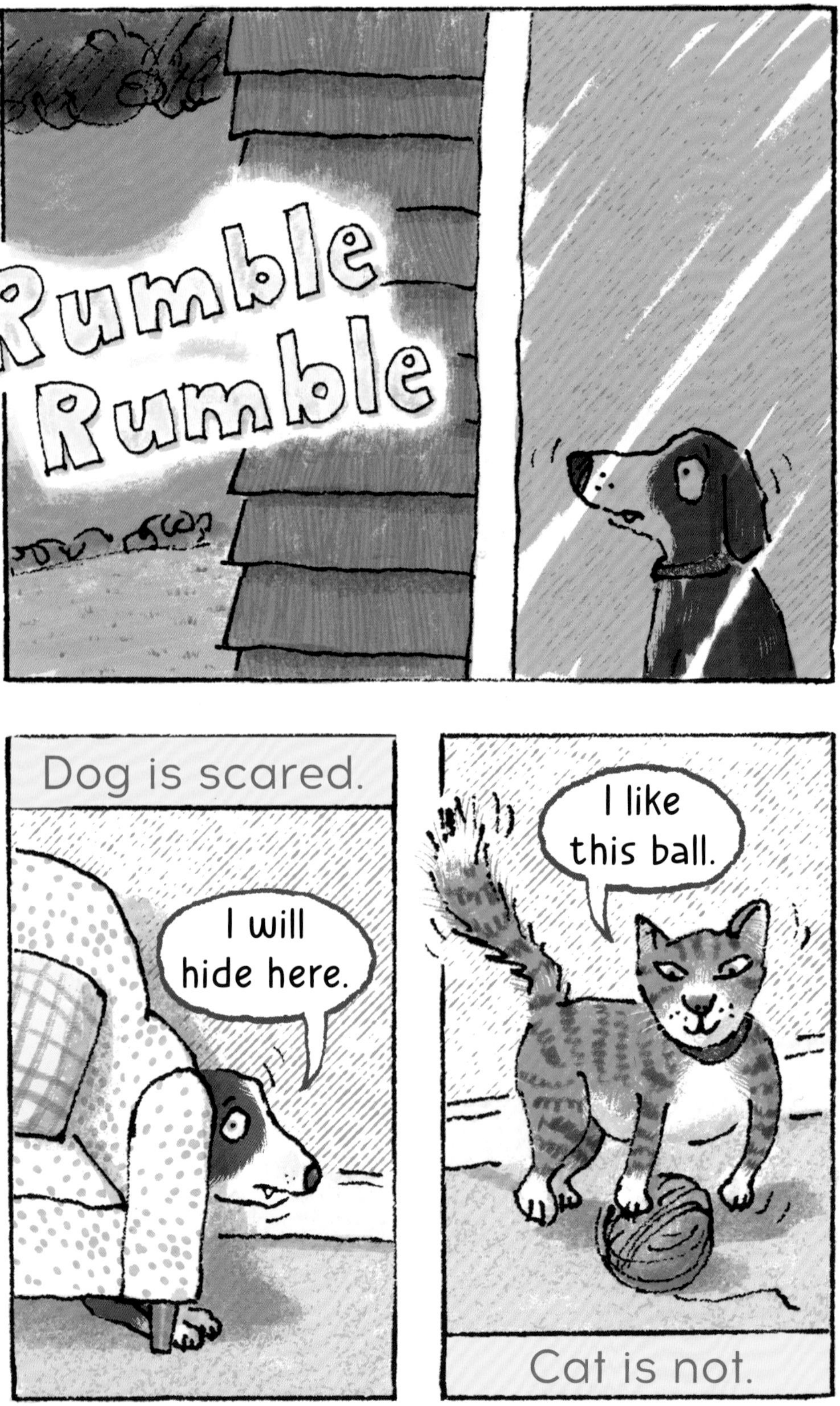
Rumble
Rumble
Dog is scared.
I will hide here.
I like this ball.
Cat is not.

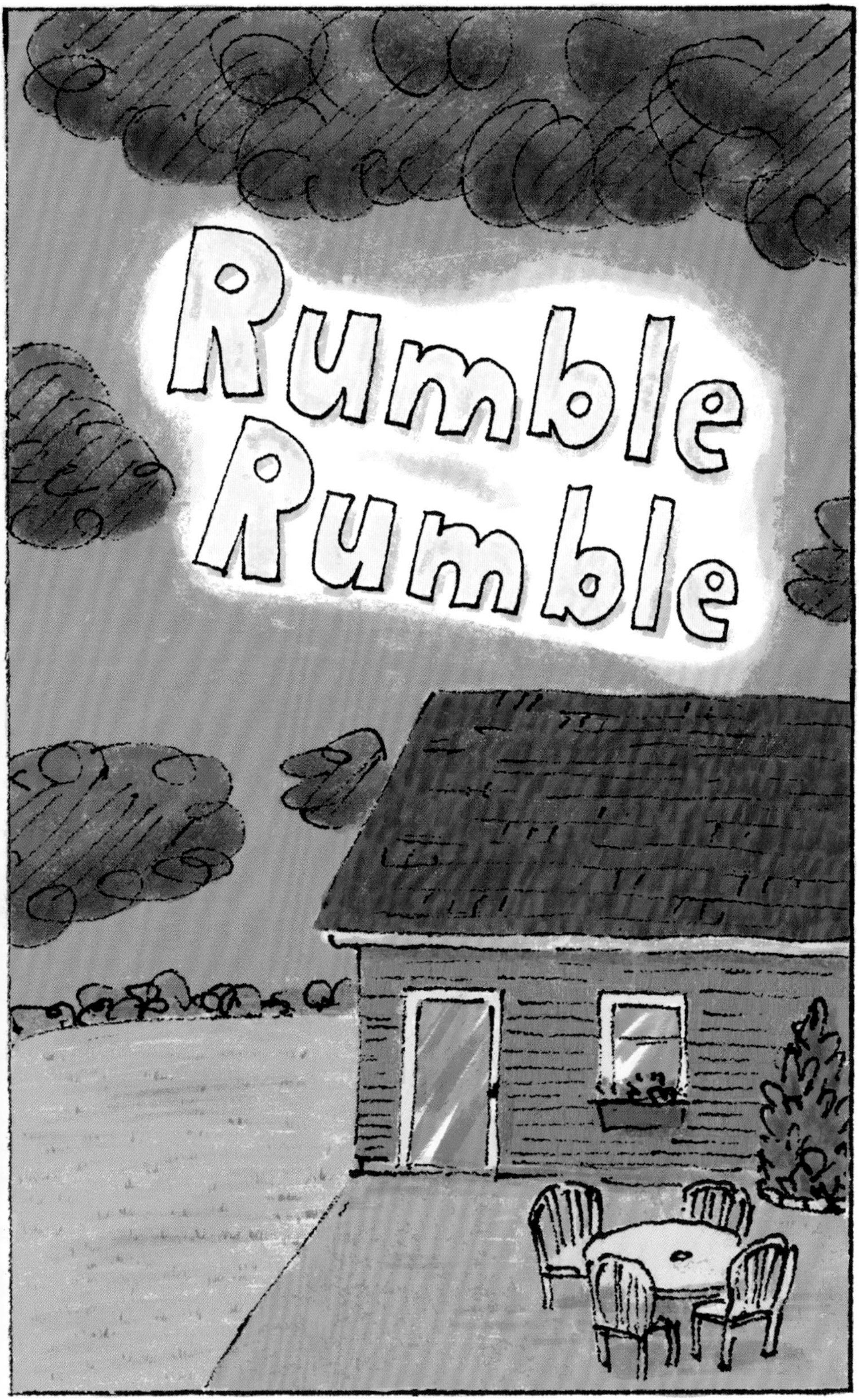
Rumble
Rumble

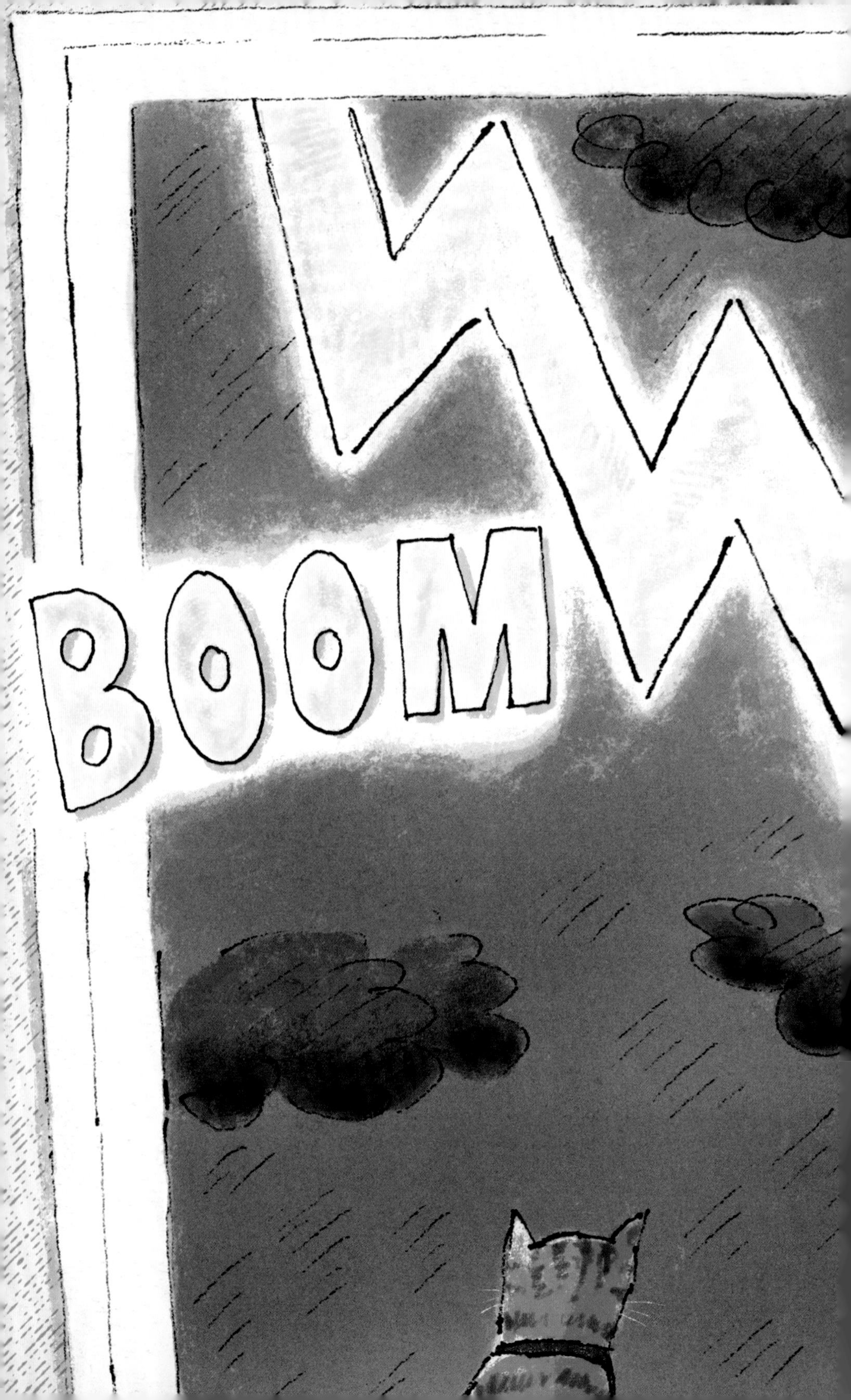
BOOM

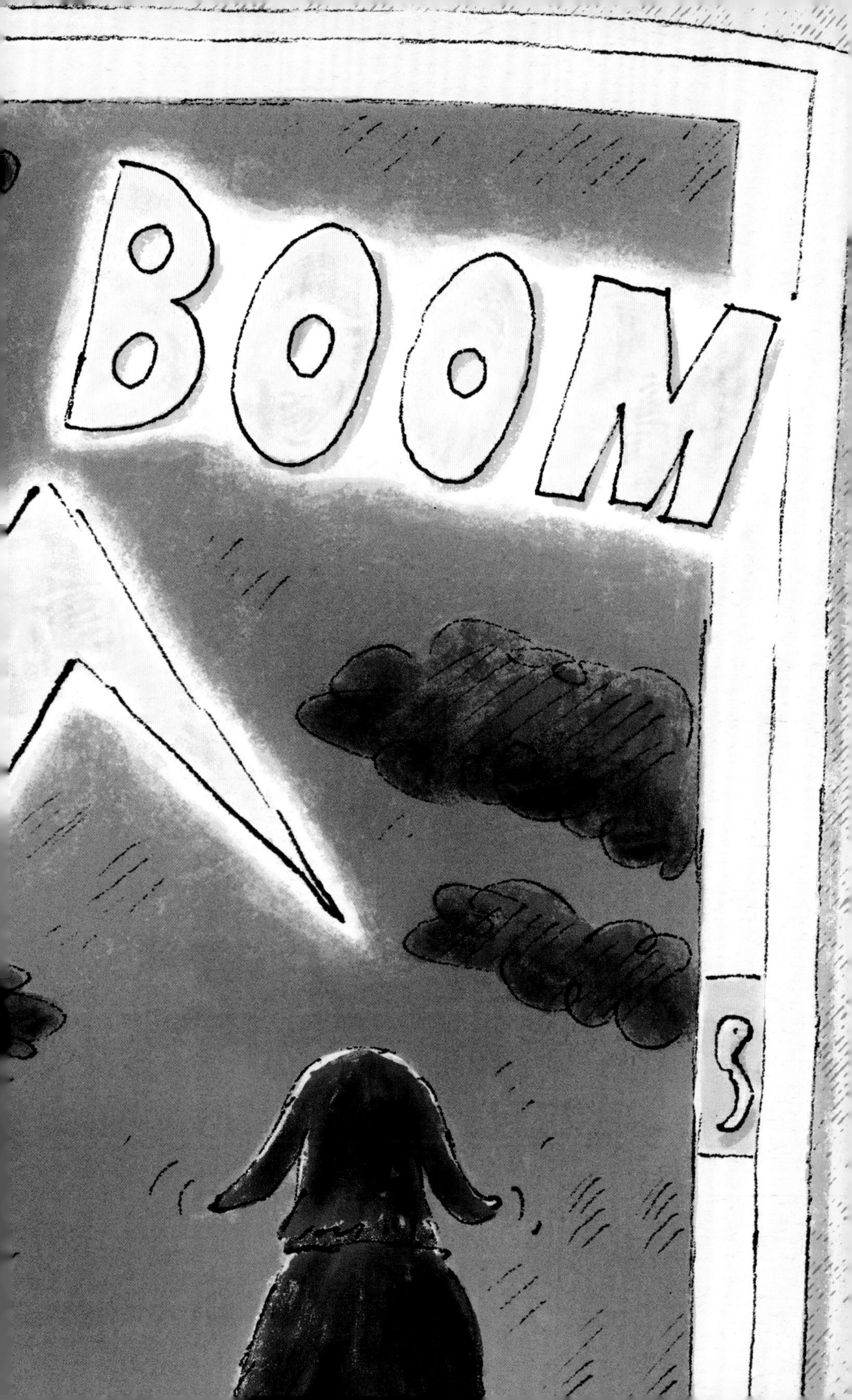
BOOM

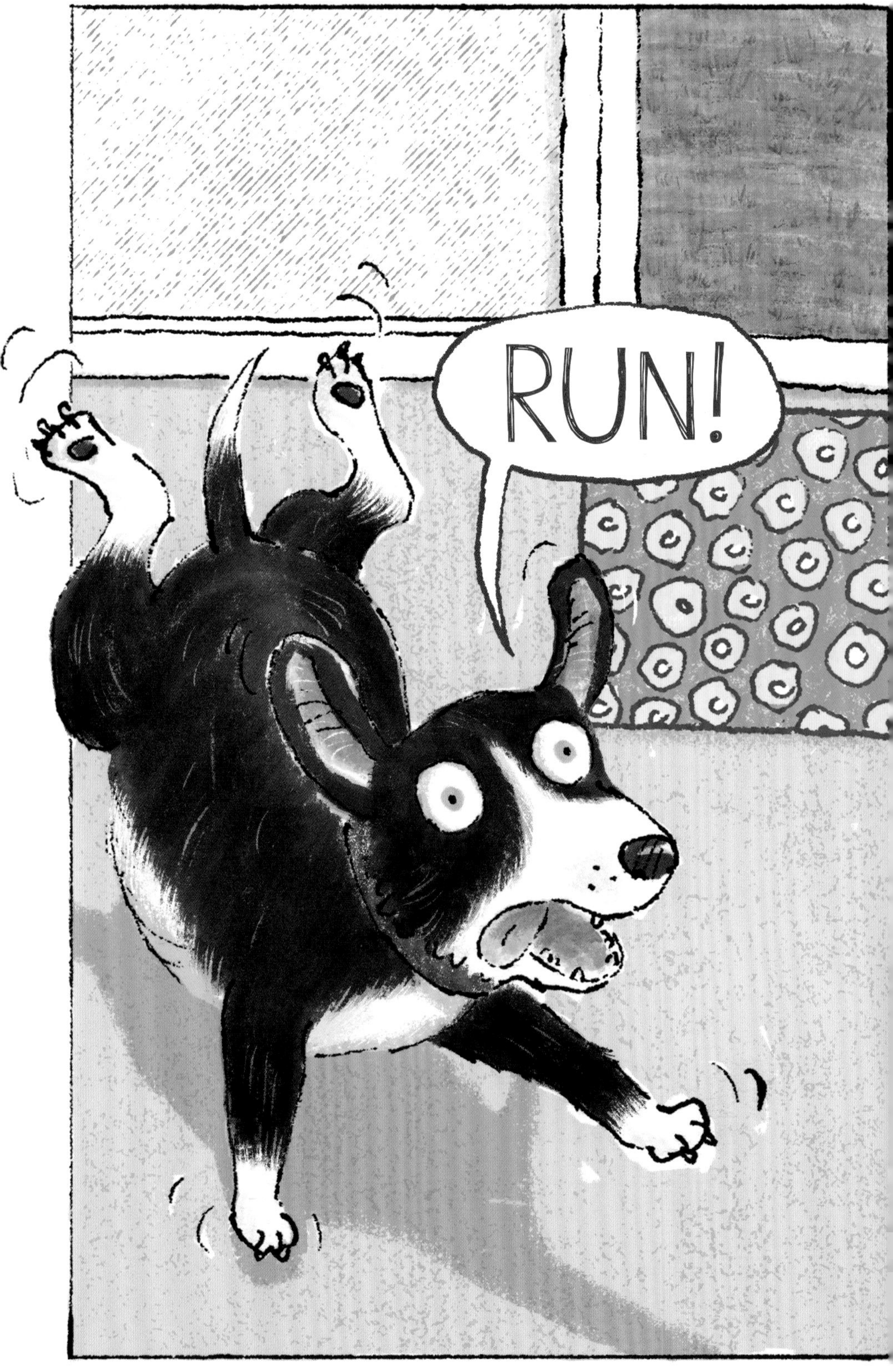
RUN!

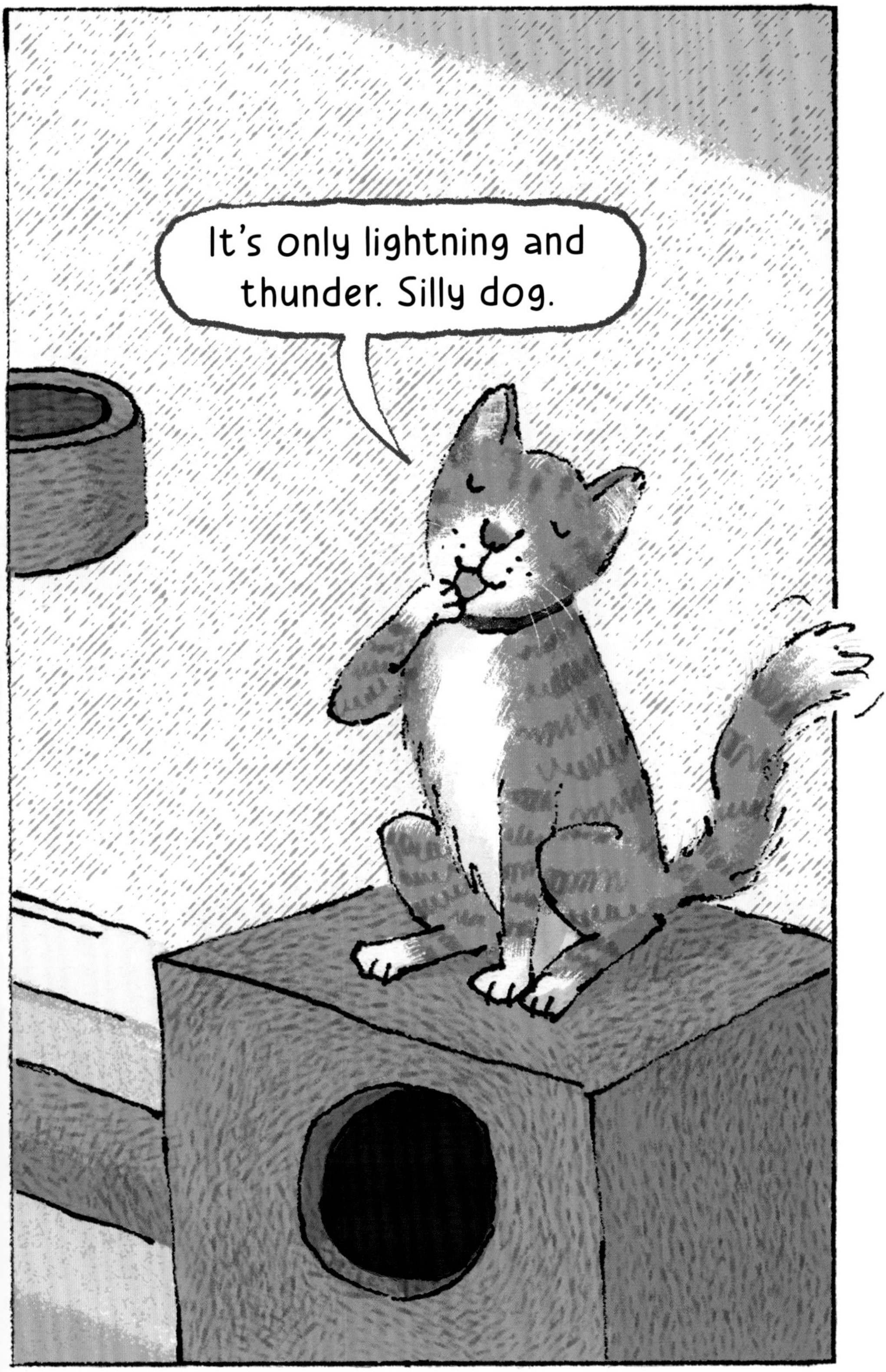
It's only lightning and thunder. Silly dog.

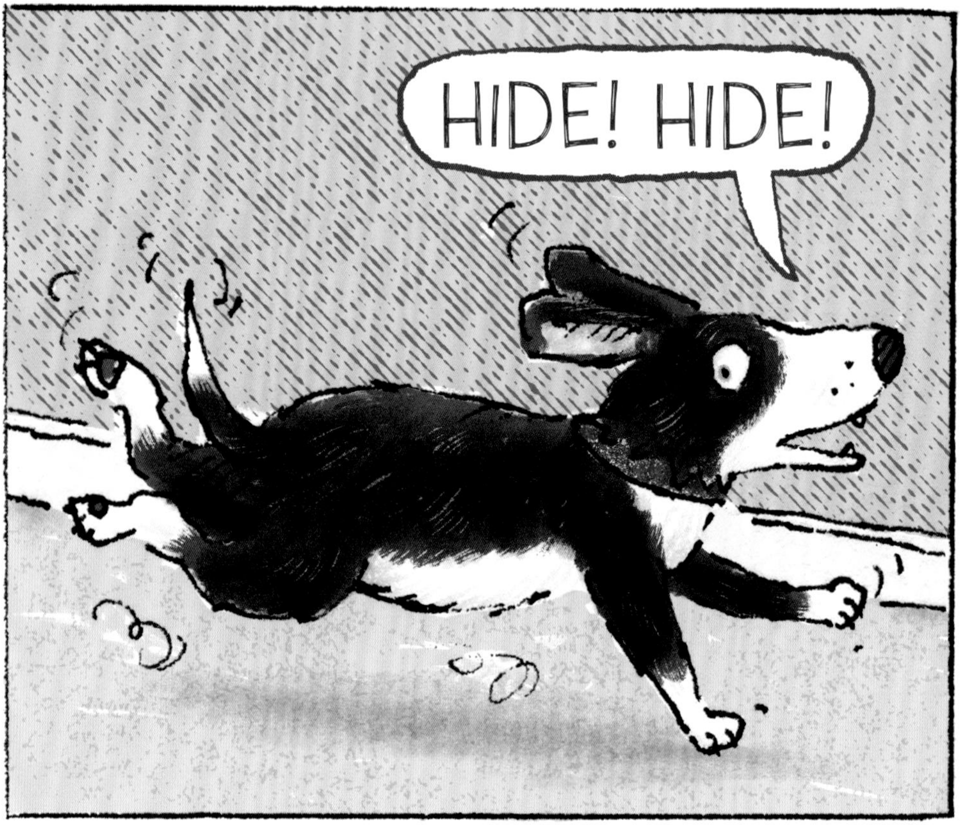
HIDE! HIDE!

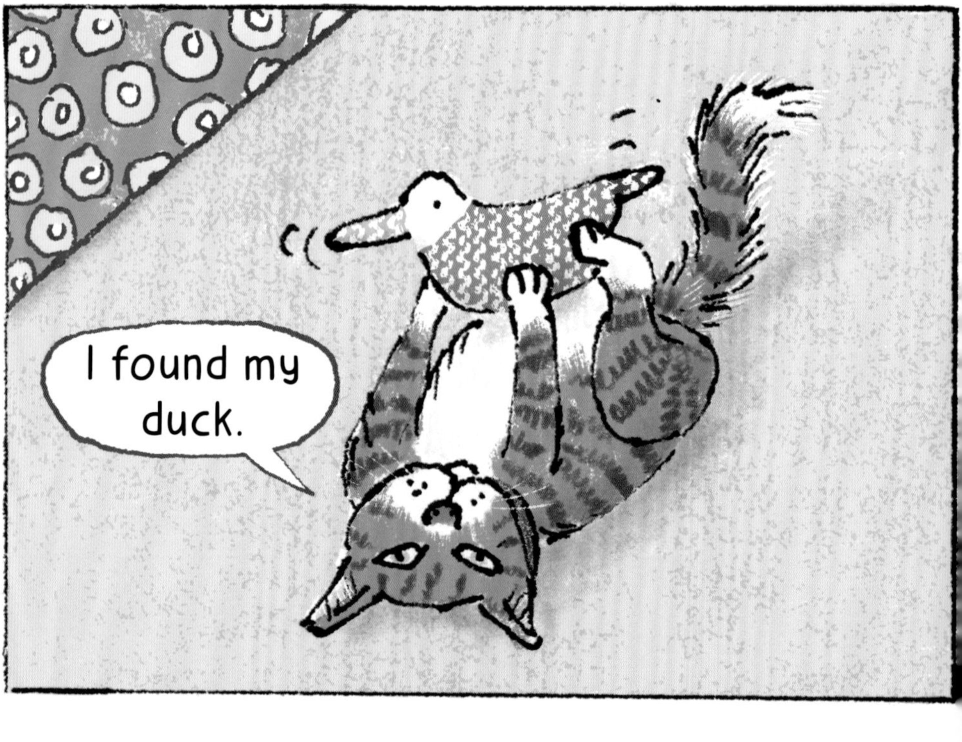
I found my duck.

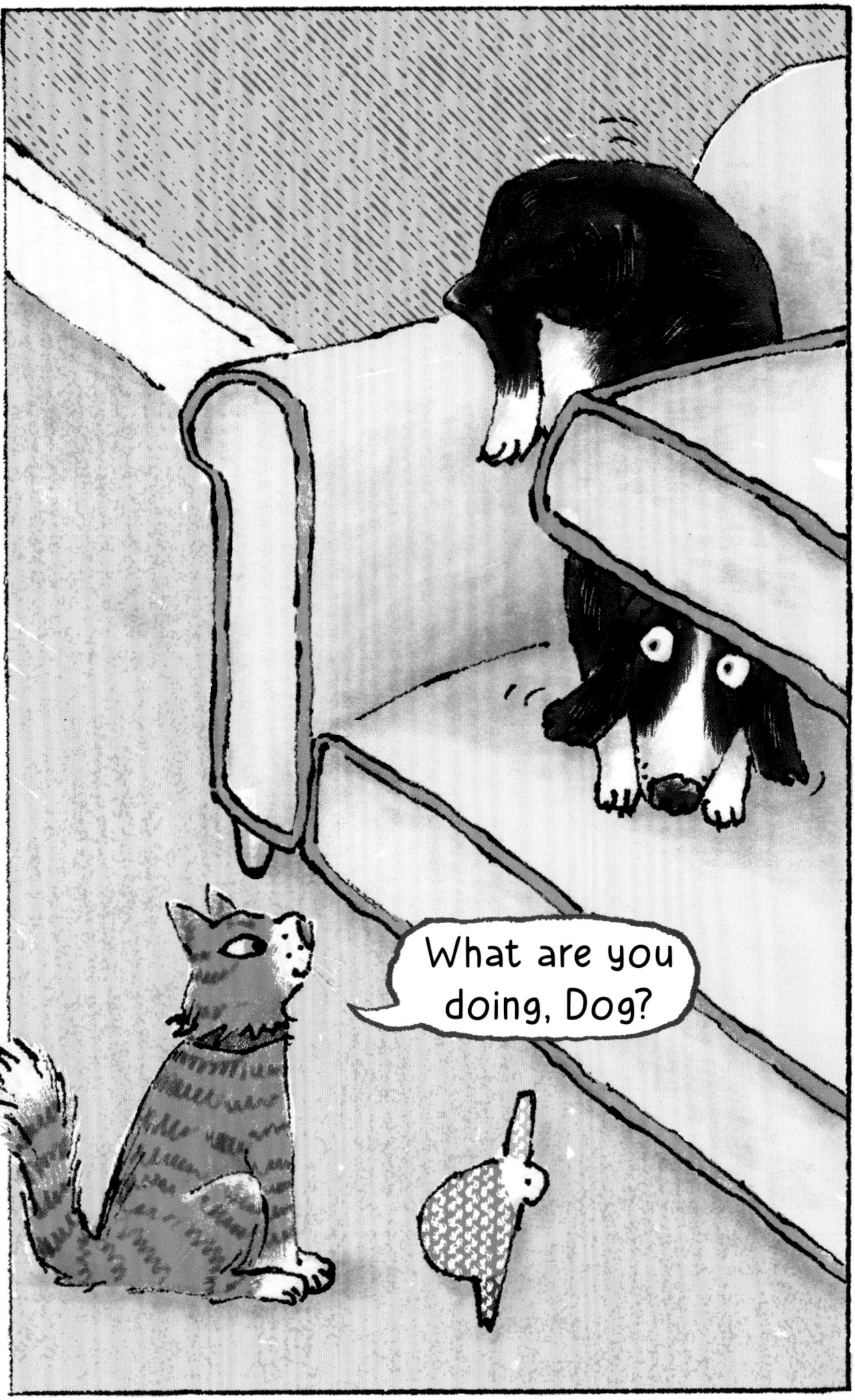
What are you doing, Dog?

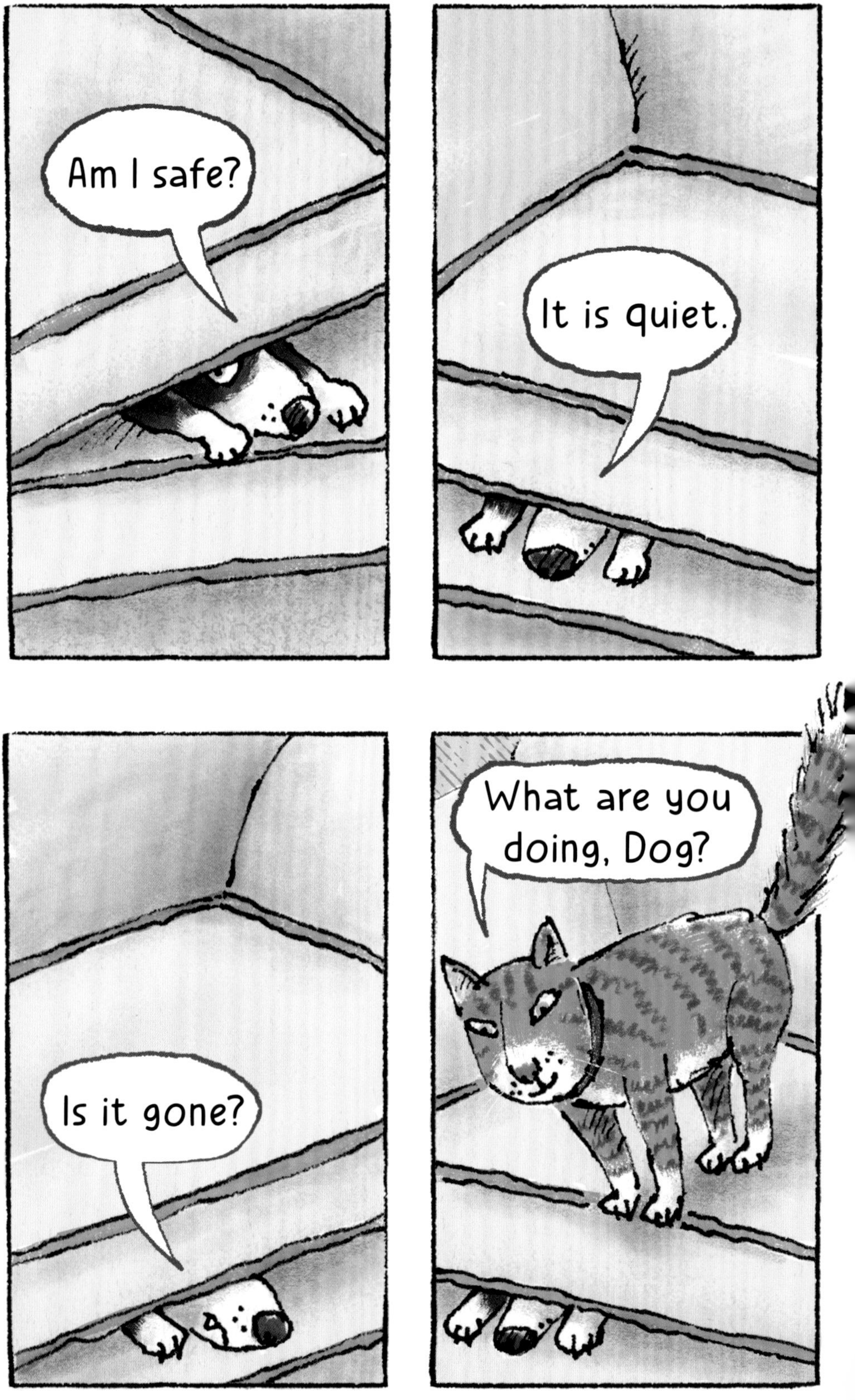
Am I safe?
It is quiet.
Is it gone?
What are you doing, Dog?

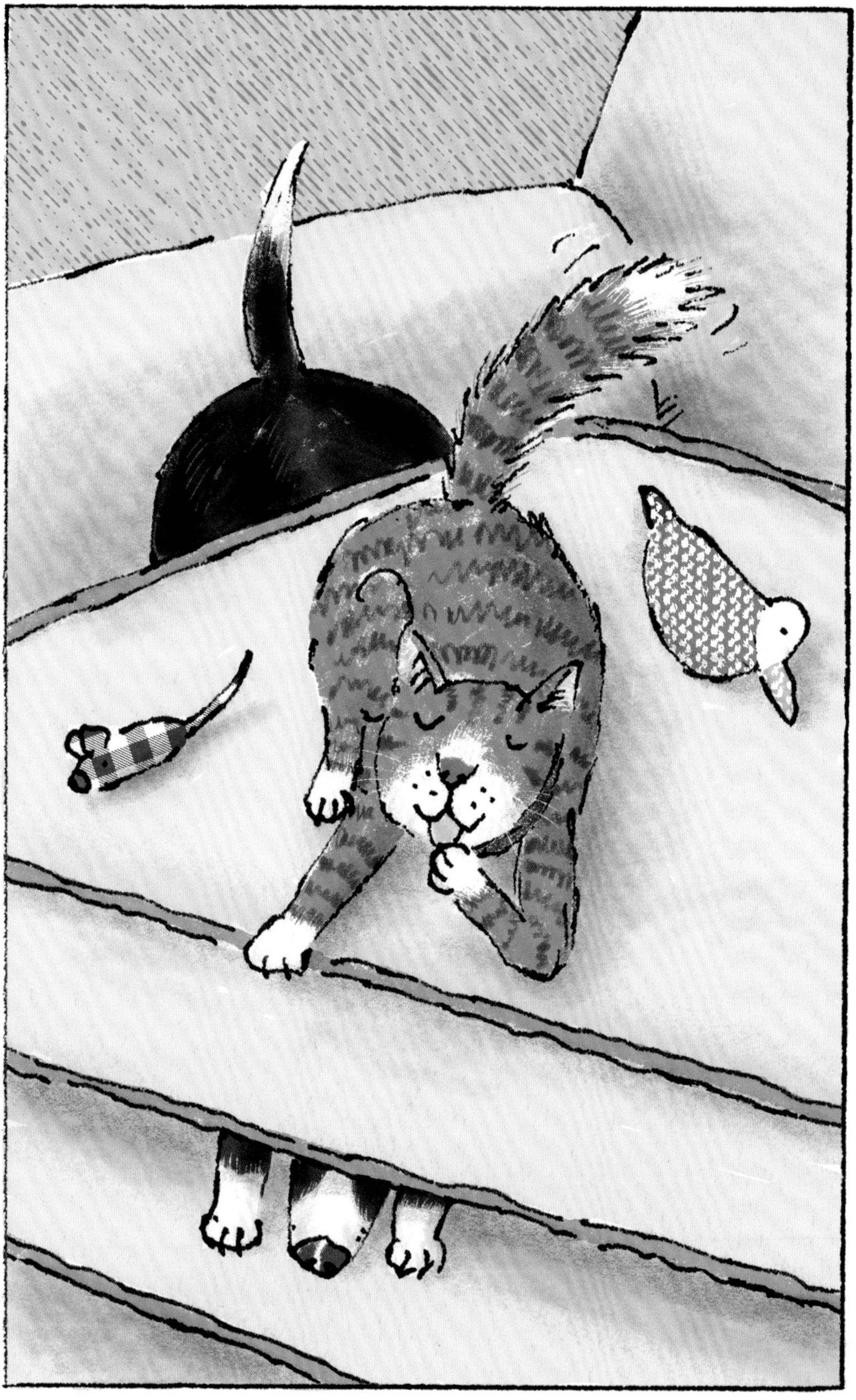

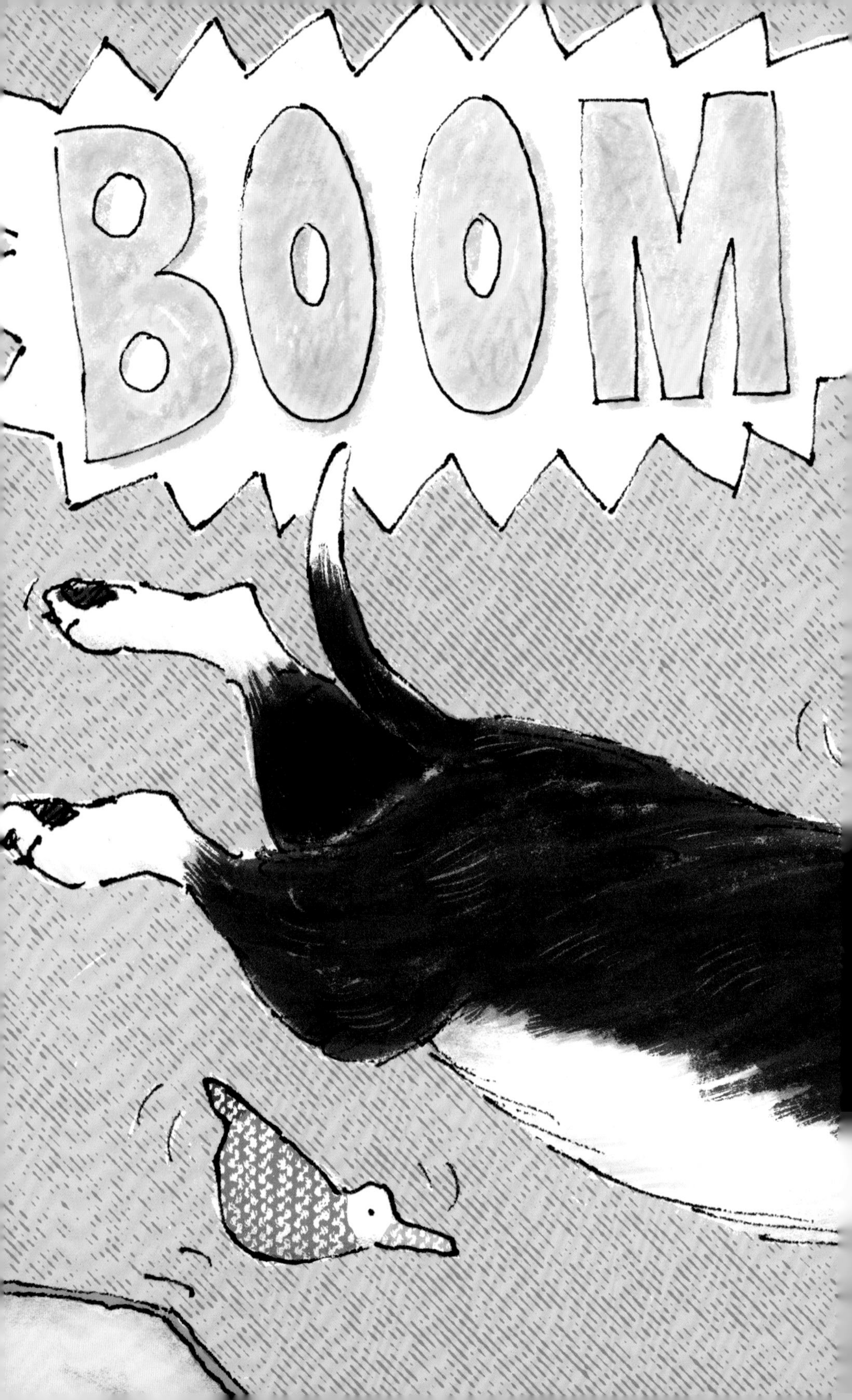
BOOM

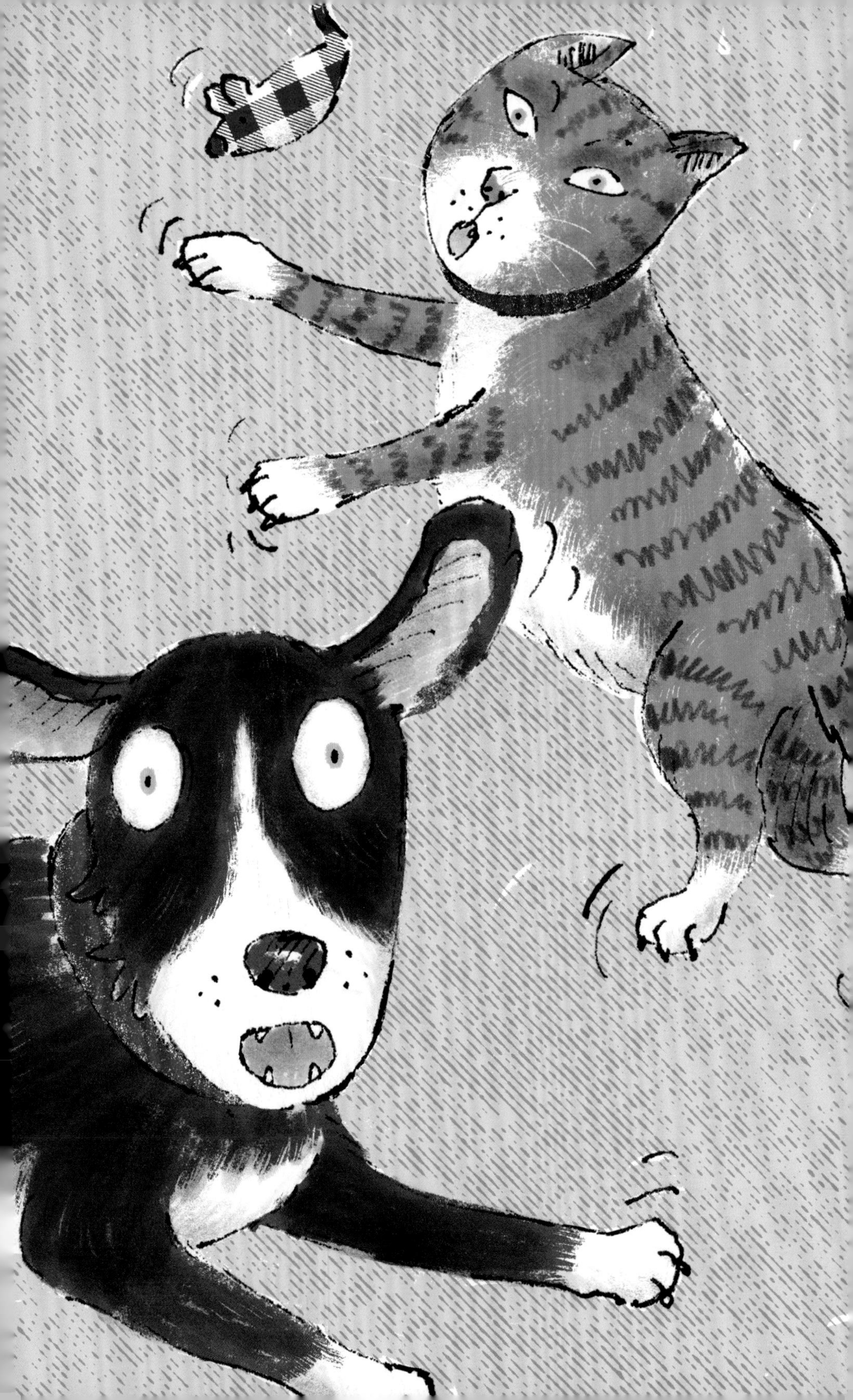

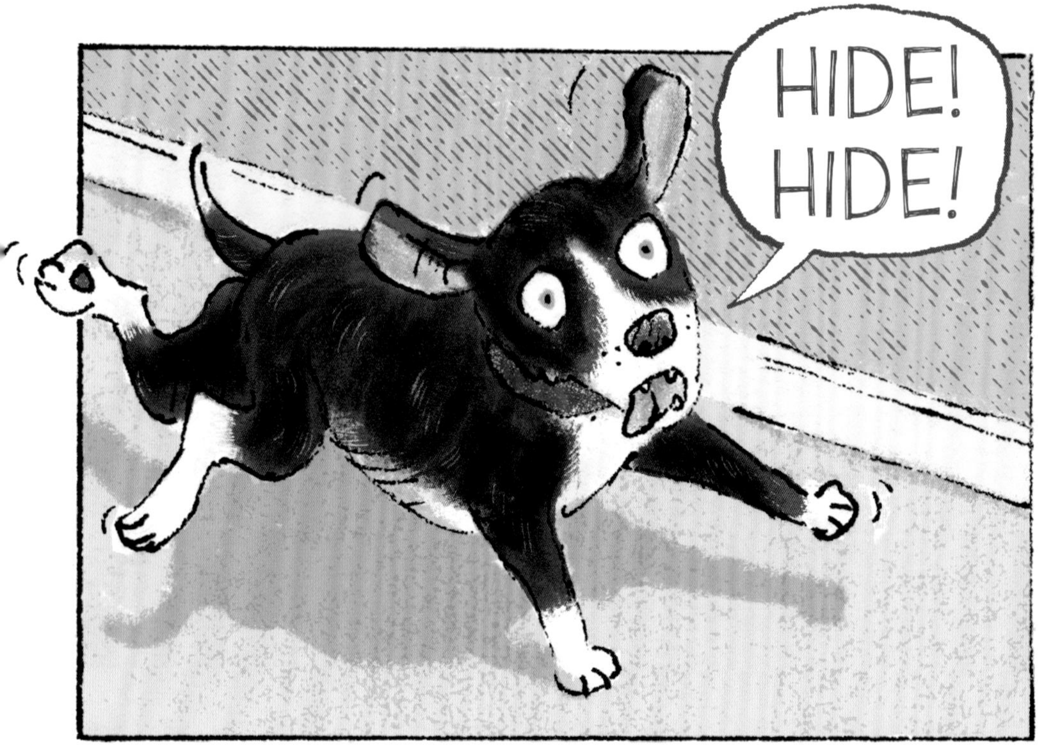
HIDE!
HIDE!

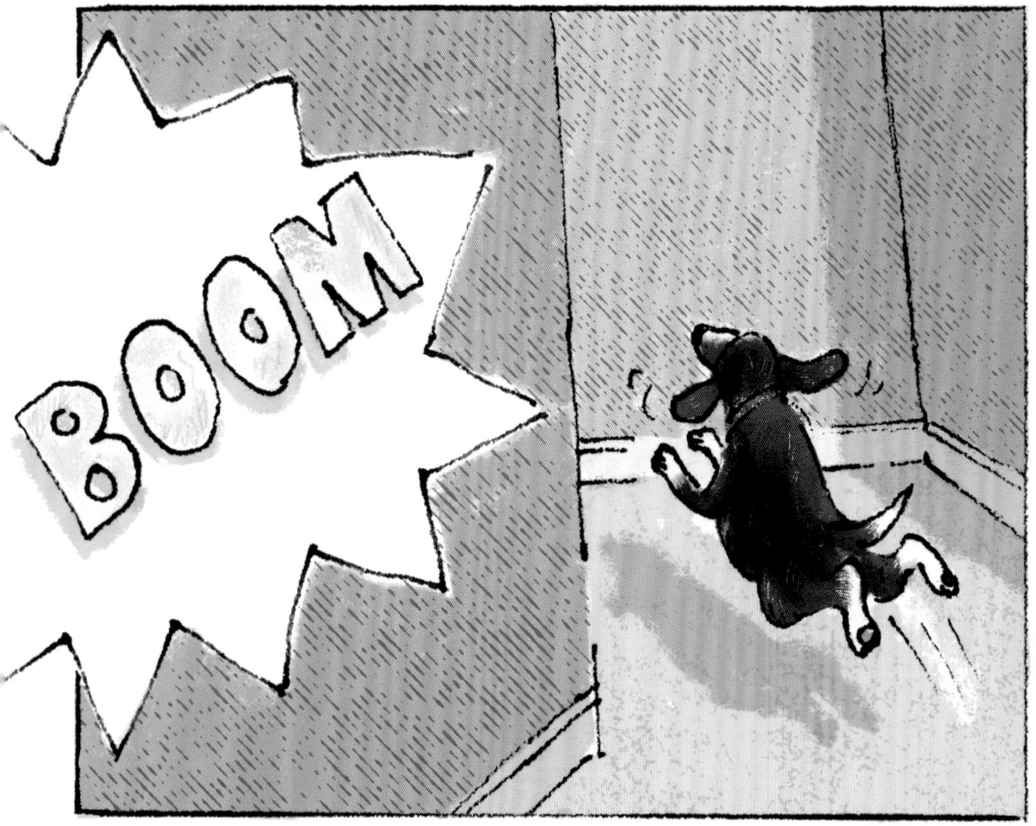
BOOM

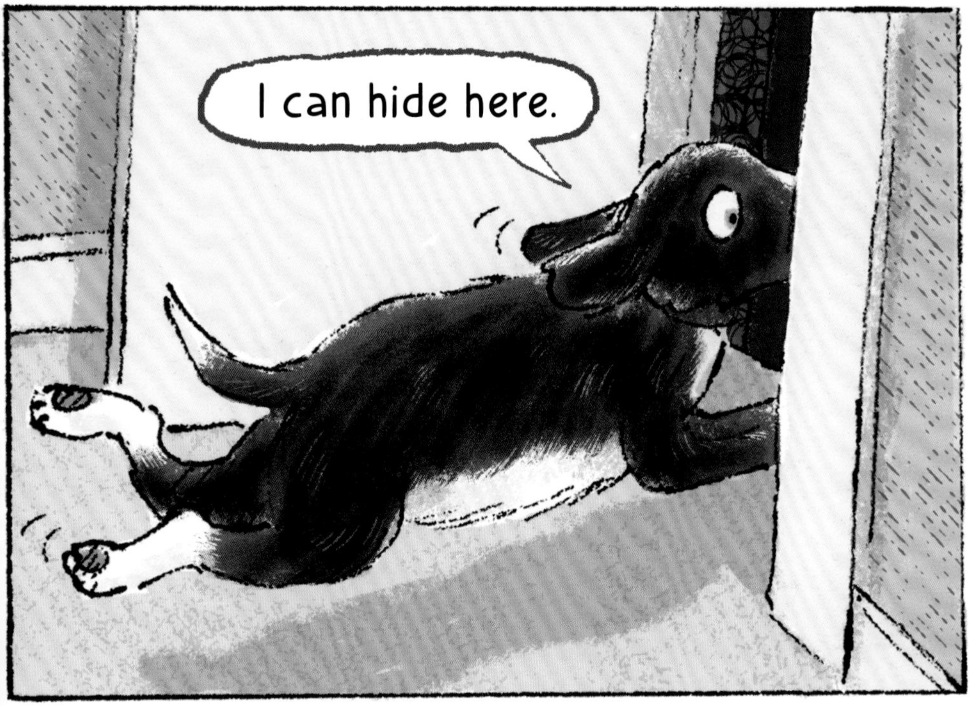
I can hide here.

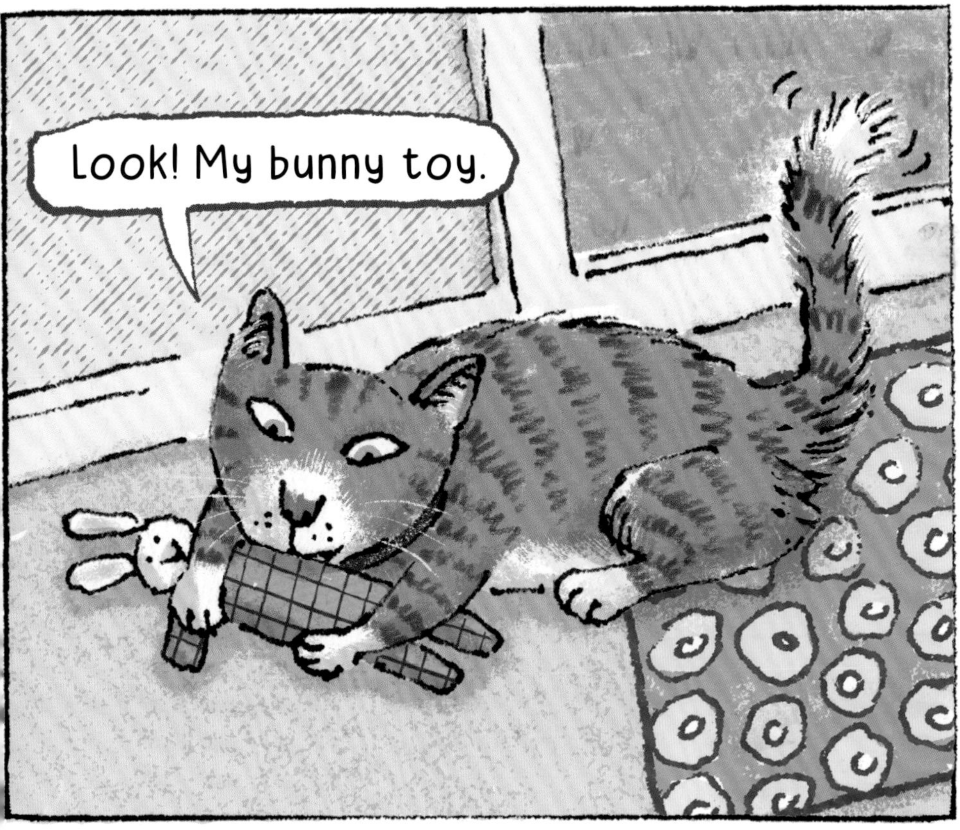
Look! My bunny toy.

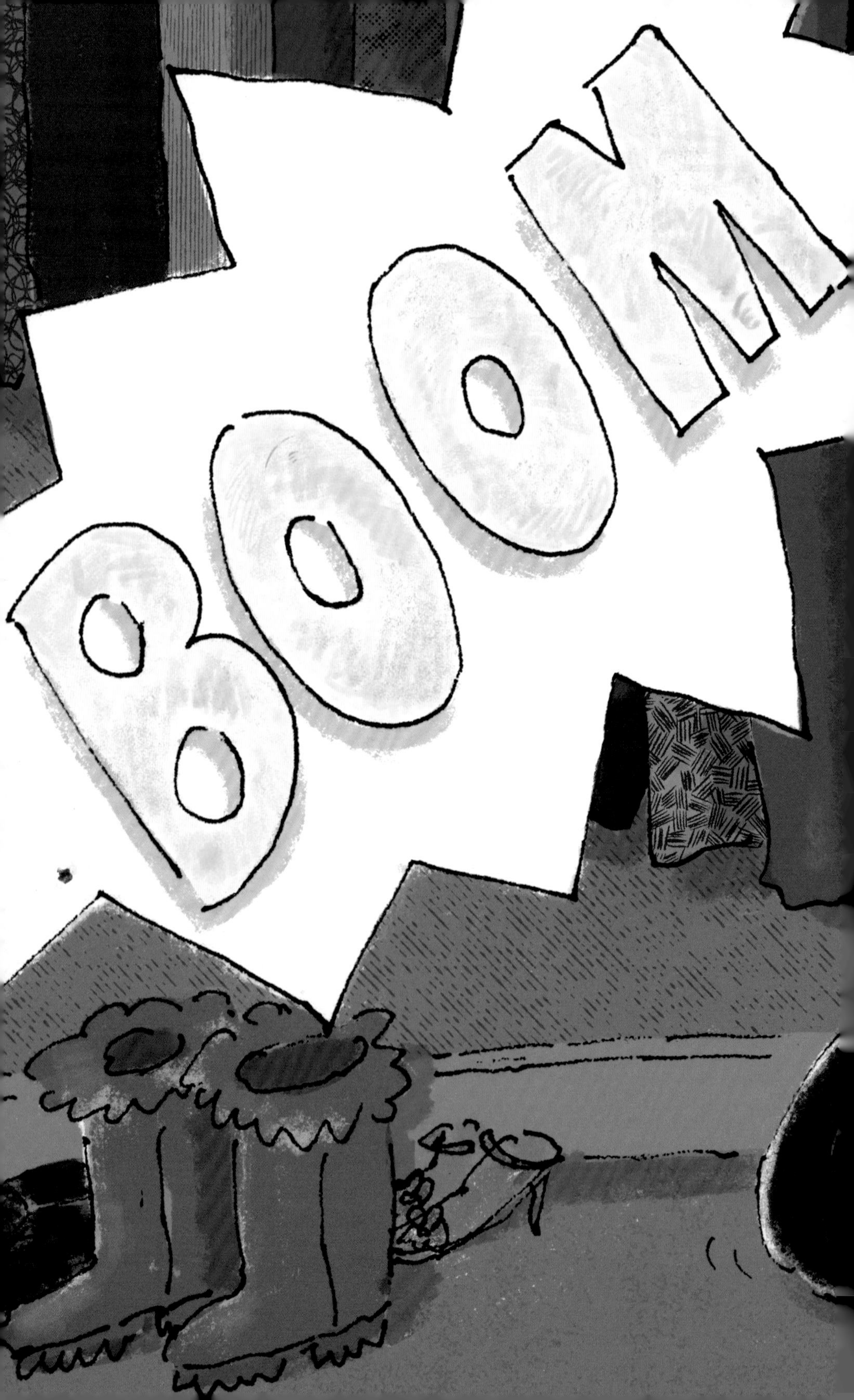
BOOM

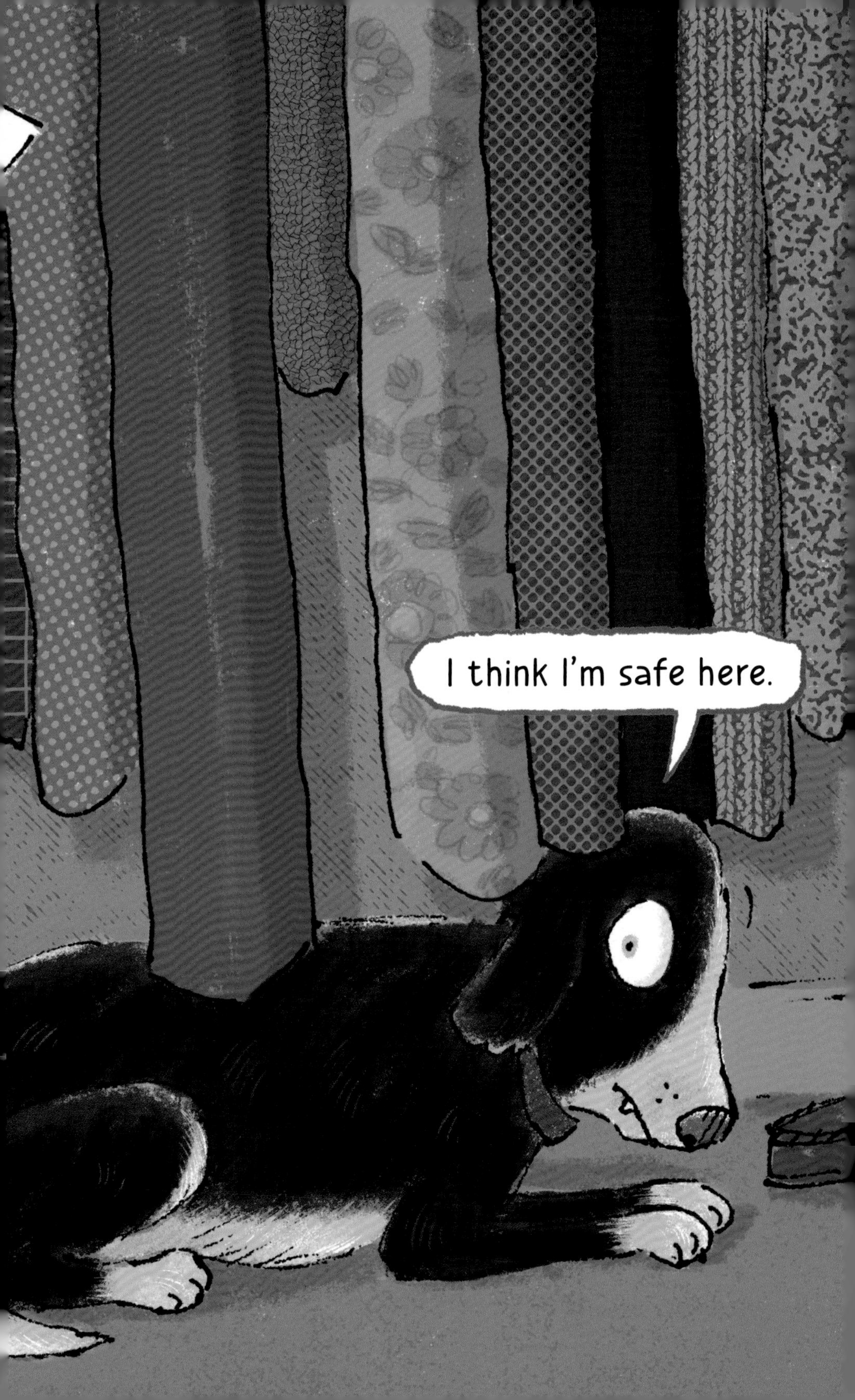
I think I'm safe here.

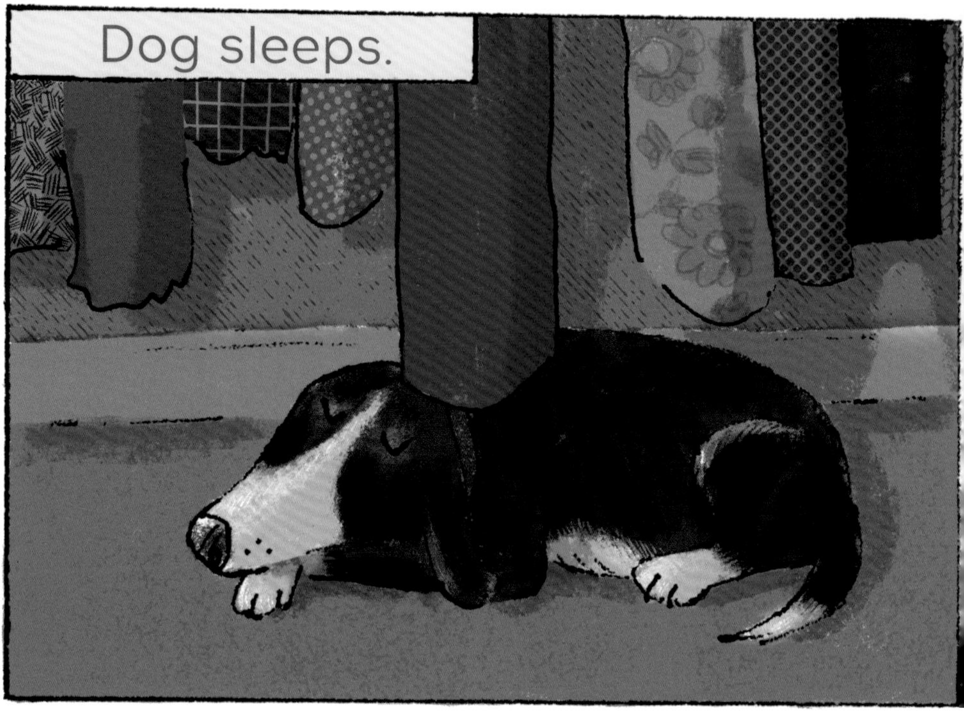
Dog sleeps.

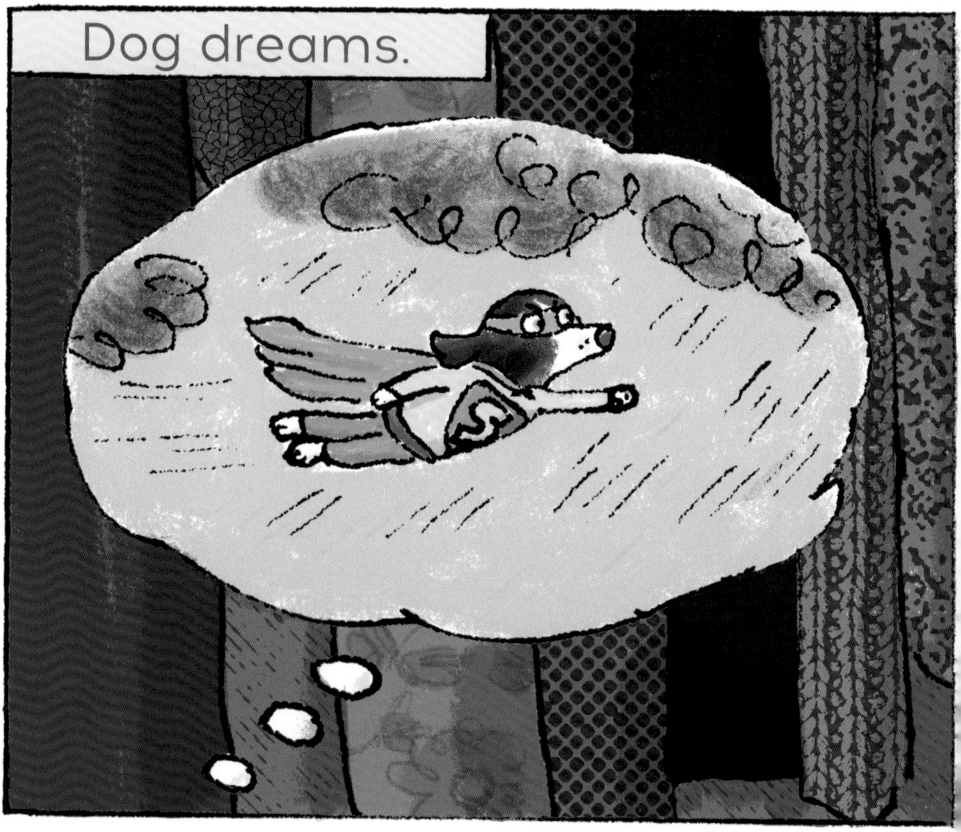
Dog dreams.

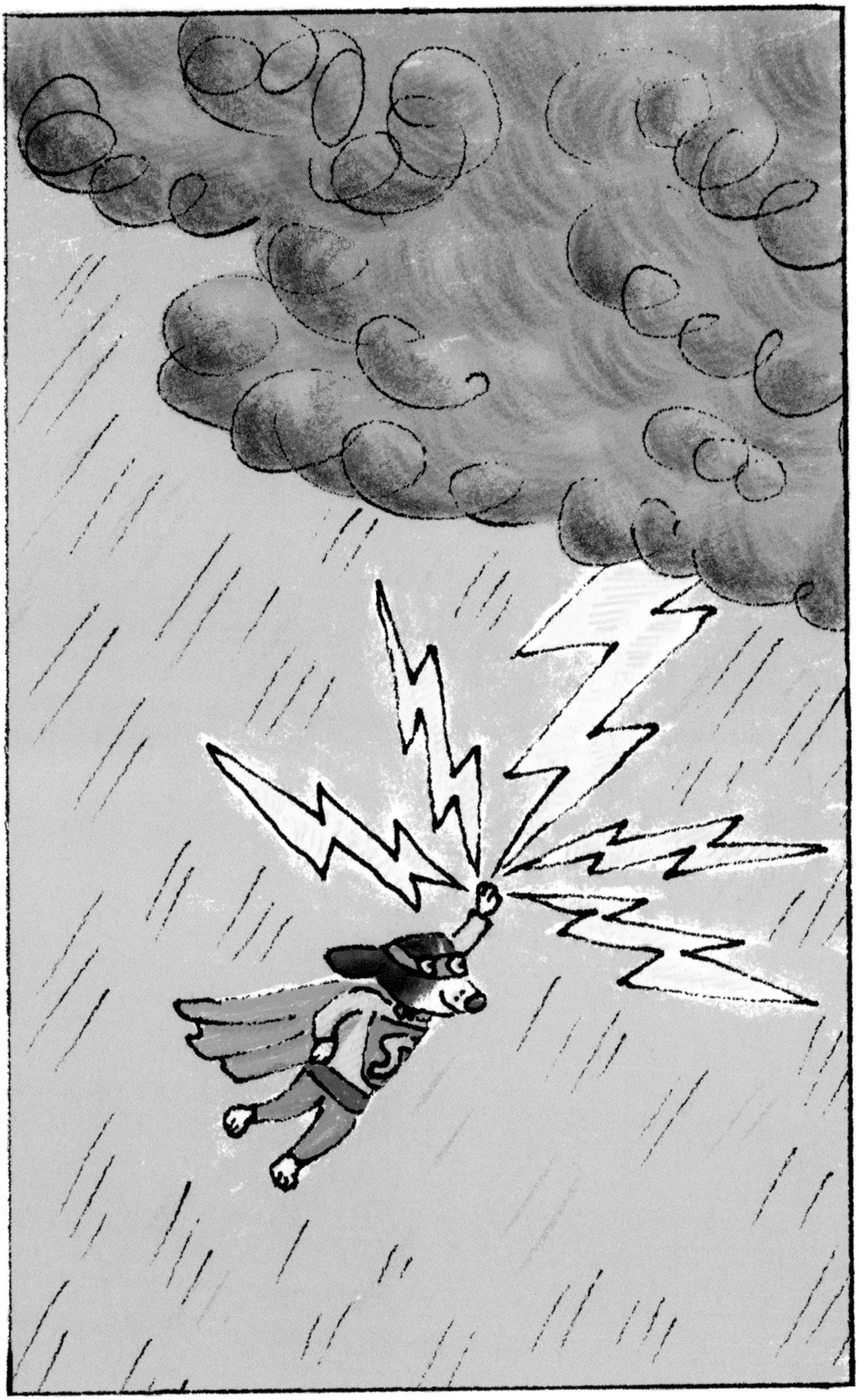

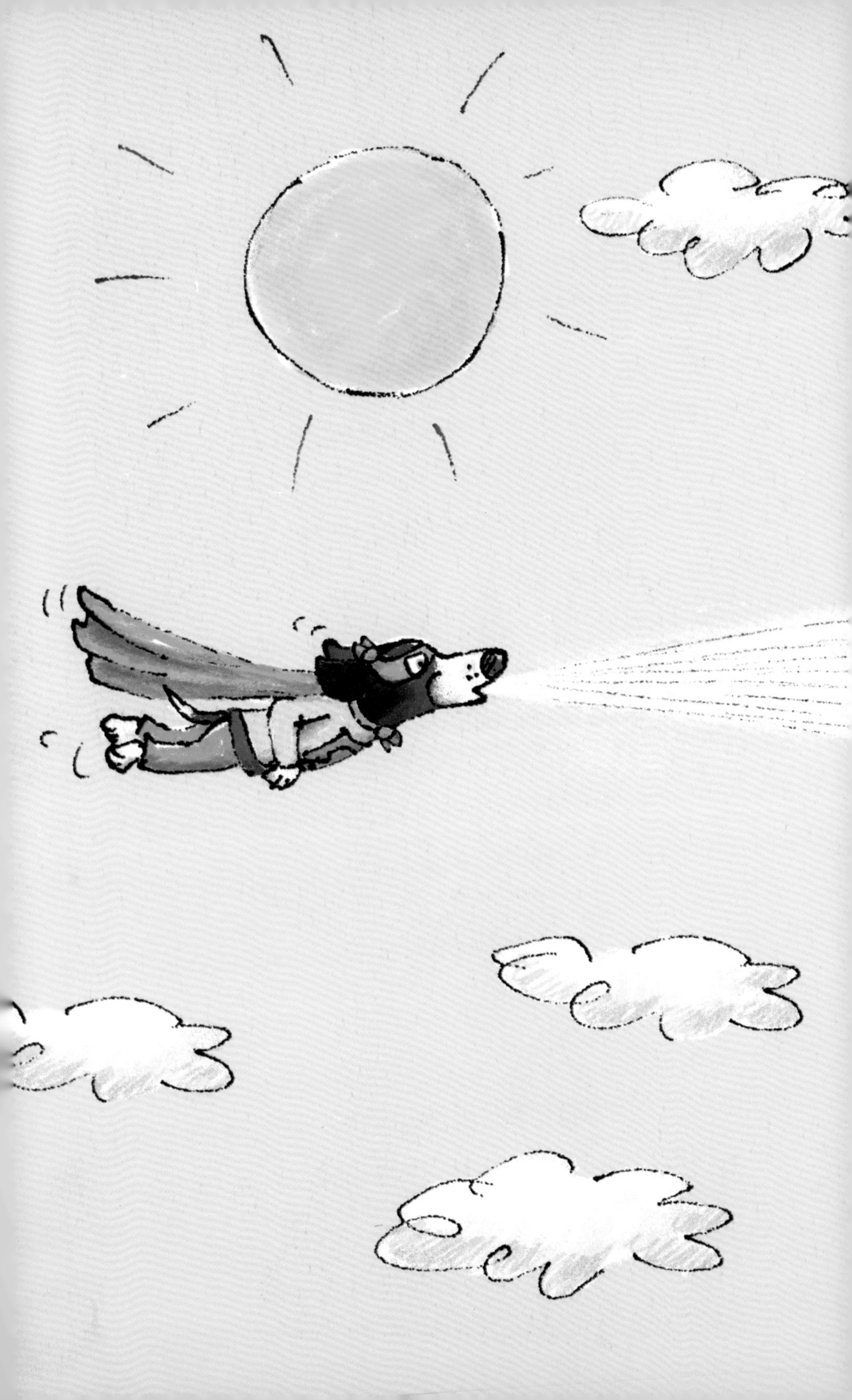

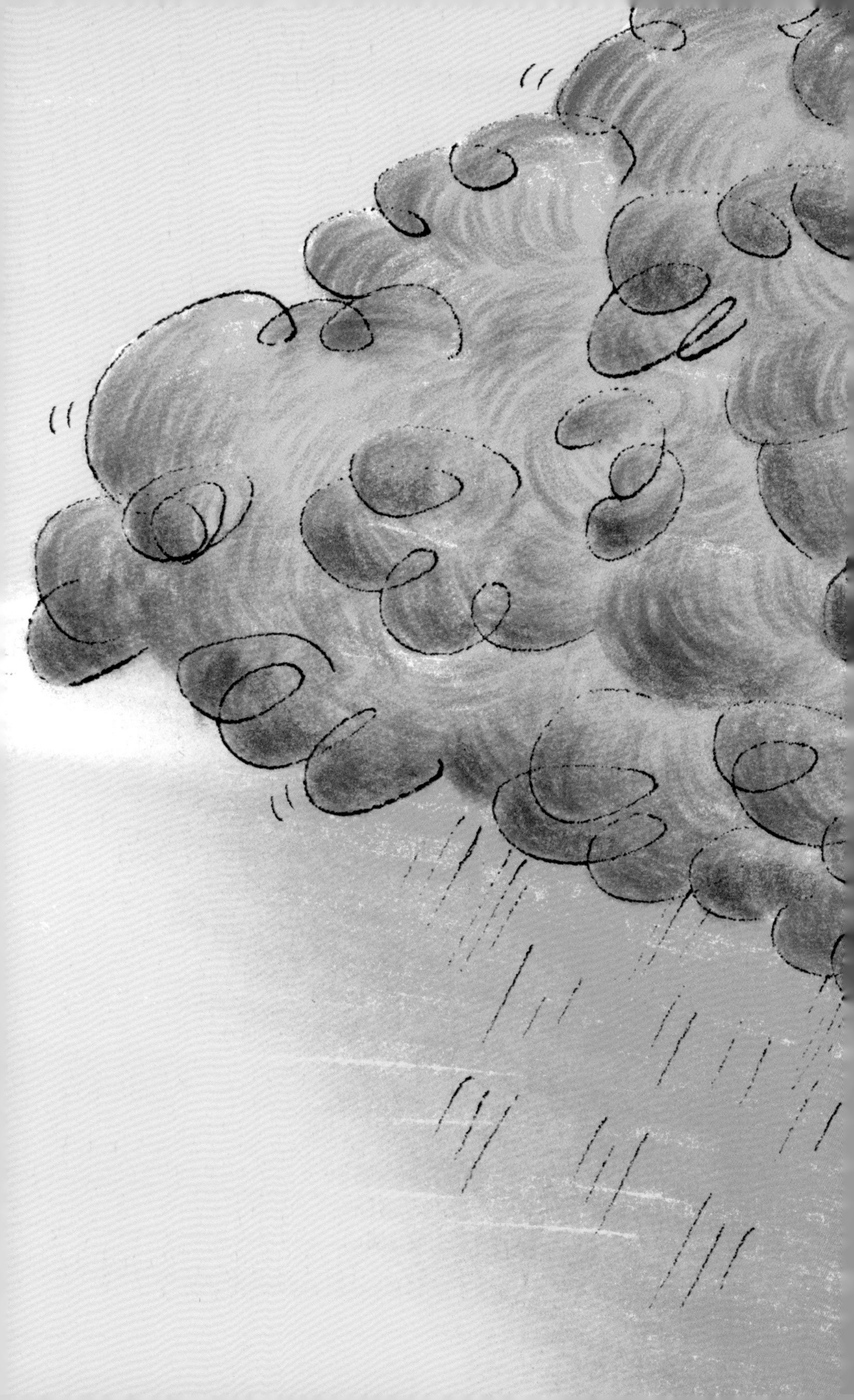

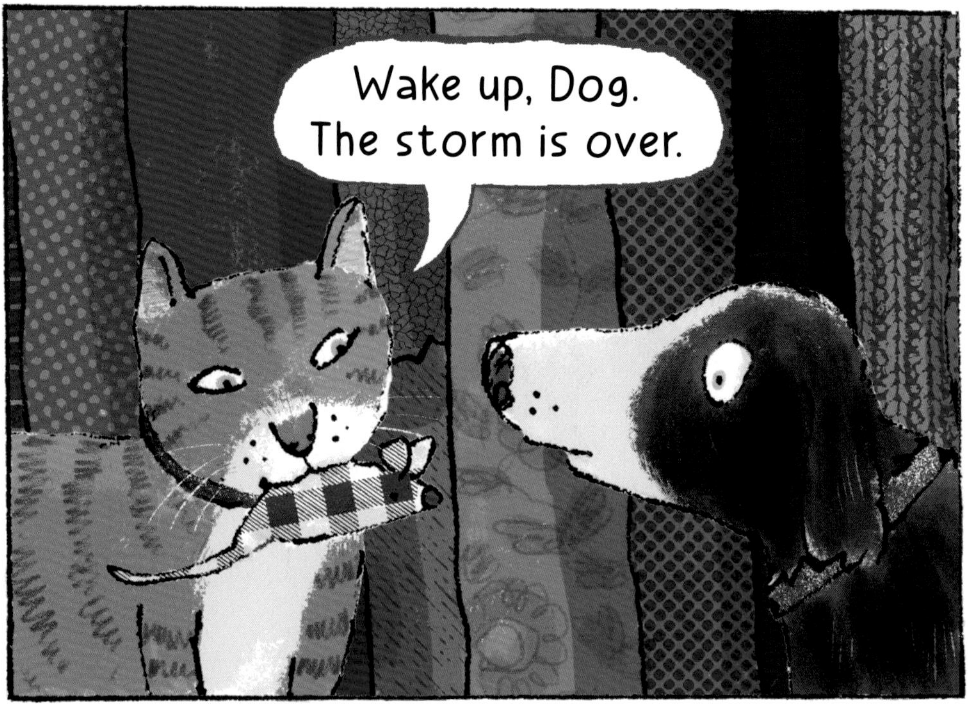
Wake up, Dog.
The storm is over.

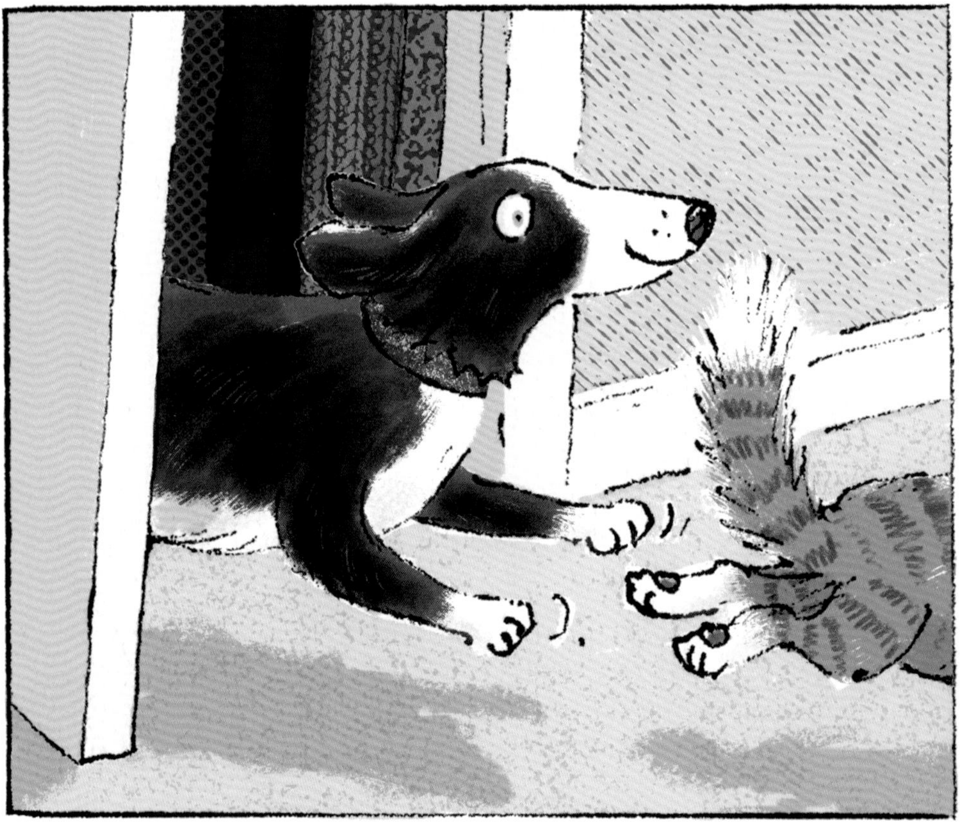

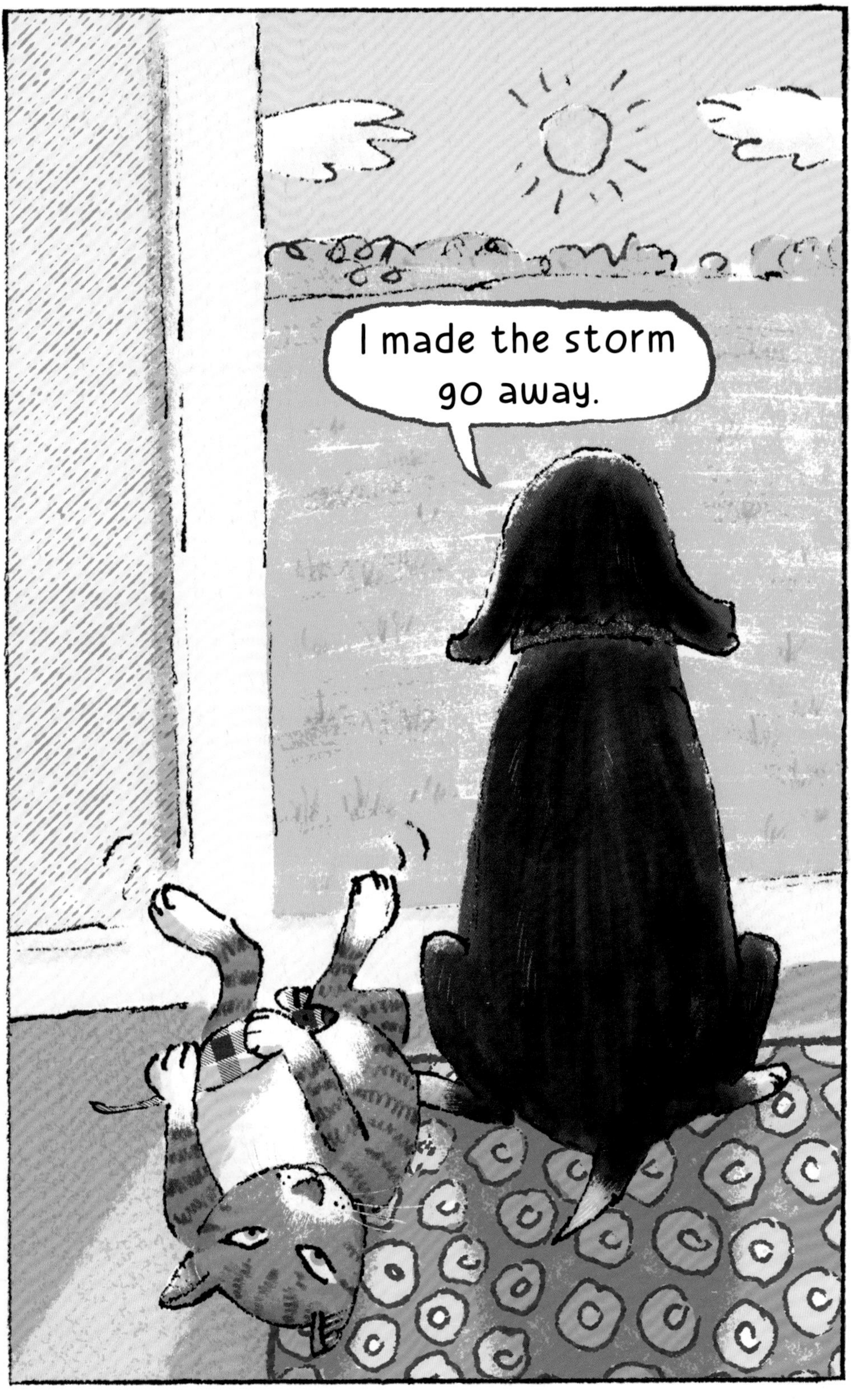
I made the storm go away.

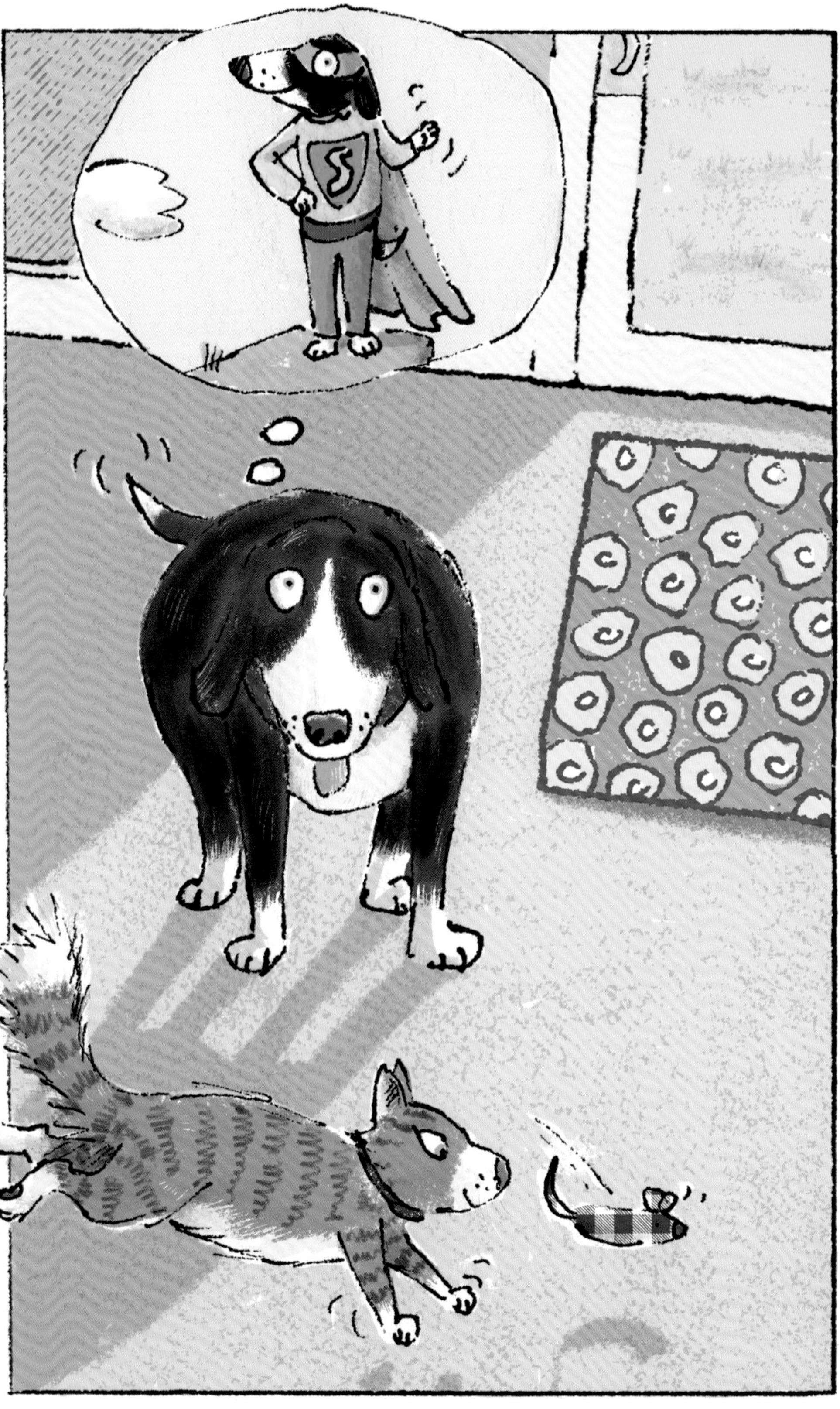

You Will Also Like

Frog and Ball
I Like to Read® COMICS
KATHY CAPLE

Ethan Long
I Like to Read® COMICS
HOGGY WENT-A-COURTIN'
42

MEET THE SUPER DUPER SEVEN
I Like to Read® COMICS™
TIM HAMILTON

I Like to Read® COMICS
I Did It!
Michael Emberley

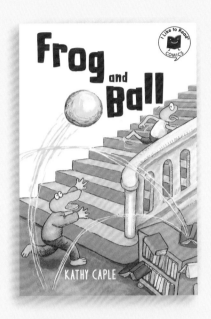

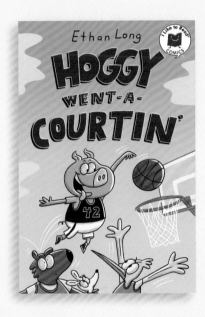

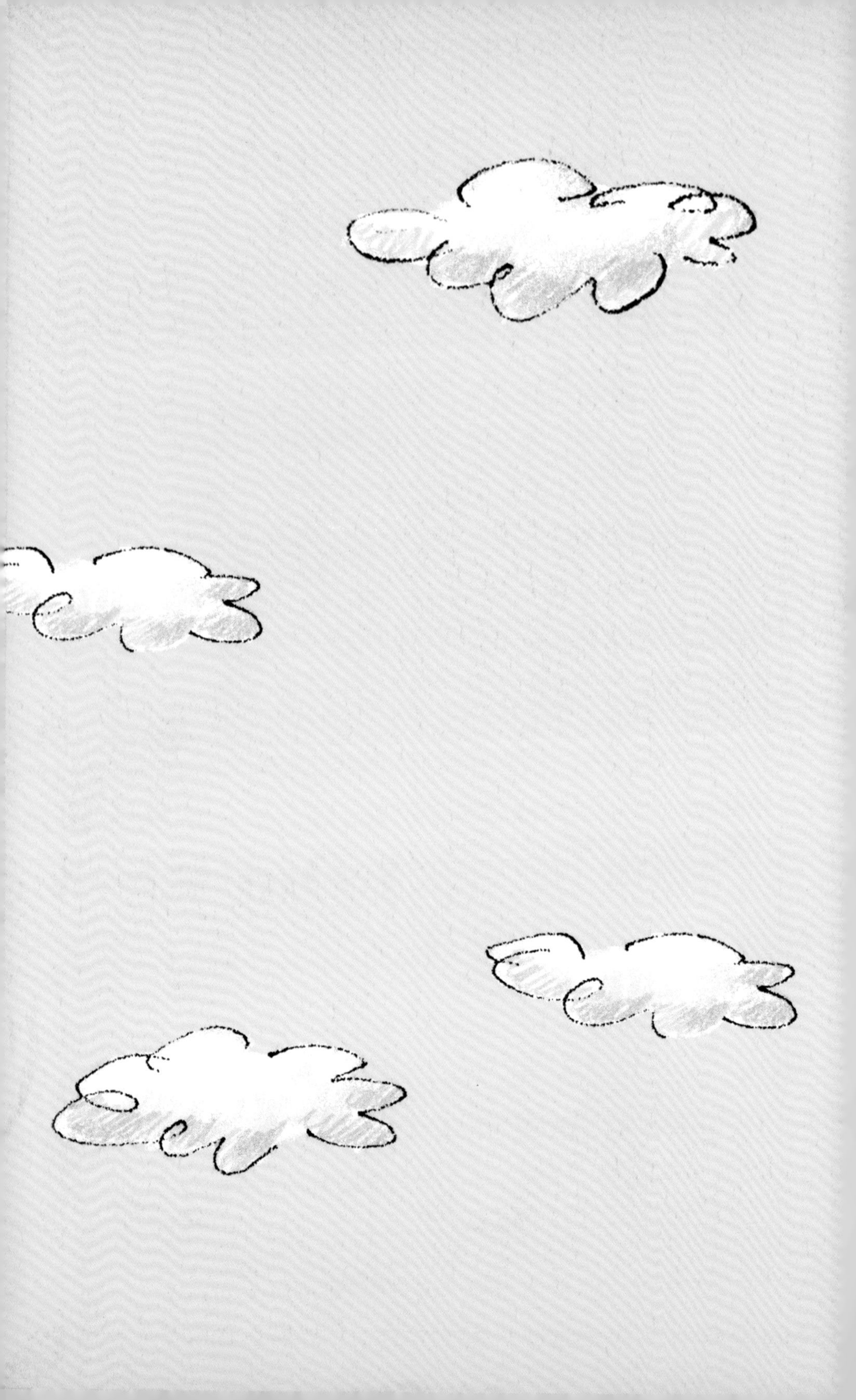